A

A STORM IS
coming

ORION AZURE

First Edition

Cover Design by Lori Rivera

Formatting by N.J. Weeks

Editing by In The Shadows Editing

CONTENTS

PLAYLIST

Goosebumps by HVME
Paradise by MEDUZA, Dermot Kennedy
I Want It All by Cameron Grey
Bring That Fire by WAR*HALL
Super Villain by Stileto, Silent Child, Kendyle Paige
Such a Whore by JVLA
RUNRUNRUN by Dutch Melrose
Where The Lights Are Low by Toby Romeo, Felix Jaehn,
FAULHABER
Mad World by Timmy Trumpet, Gabry Ponte
Fearless Pt II by Lost Sky, Chris Linton
Trouble by Camylio
Mercy by Hurts
Cravin' by Stileto, Kendyle Paige
It's No Good by The Nocturnal Affair
House of Balloons/Glass Table Girls by The Weeknd
The Death of Peace of Mind by Bad Omens
Memories by David Guetta, Kid Cudi
So Alive by No Resolve

Killing Me Slowly by Bad Wolves
Just Pretend by Bad Omens
Closer by Nine Inch Nails

To those looking to be chased in the woods and fucked by three masked men...
This is definitely for you!

TRIGGER WARNINGS

Includes but not limited to...
Forced Proximity
Masked Men
Non-Consensual
CNC
Primal
Degradation
Bondage
Knife Play

1

SKYLAN

"So, what plans do you have for winter break?" Kenzi asks me, as we walk to the parking lot outside of the recreation center. The freezing wind cuts through the open space, tossing my chocolate brown hair everywhere, chilling me to my core. My wavy hair always looks in disarray, but this wind definitely doesn't help. I tighten the hold I have on the books I'm holding to my chest trying to stave off the frigid weather.

The campus isn't as busy today and the sparse vehicles around the parking lot shows that, especially since most of the students have already left for winter break. Everyone is heading home or to their families' vacation homes for the next two weeks. Unfortunately, I can't leave just yet since my stepbrother and I are driving together, and I have to wait for Jayden to finish up with football practice.

Since Georgia Tech didn't make it to the playoffs this year, the coach made them do a final training session as punishment and to get them ready for the next year. I know how tough his coach is on them during regular practices, so this will probably be worse.

"We're heading to Gatlinburg this year," I mutter, glancing over to her. Looking down as we walk, I can tell Kenzi is a little upset. She's had a crush on Jayden for a while, even though he never notices her. I have tried to talk her up to him, but he's just not having any of it, brushing me off every time. Those discussions usually end up with him storming off and ignoring me for hours, sometimes even for days. I finally gave up trying.

"Cheer up. It's only two weeks. We will be back before you know it," I say, trying to lift her spirits. Bumping her shoulder, I say, "And we can Facetime and message while I'm there. Are you heading to your parents' house in Texas?"

She chuckles, stumbling from me bumping her. "Yeah." When she rights herself, we continue to her car. "You know how much I hate Texas. But my flight leaves in the morning. When are you guys heading out?" she asks as we near her car.

Stepping to her driver's side door, she unlocks and opens it. Tossing her bag into the passenger seat she stands up straight and leans against the door. Adjusting the books I'm holding, I cock my hip and lean against the front fender of her car. "I don't know. Whenever Jayden is out of practice," I say, glancing over my shoulder at where I know he and the team will be coming from. "We're taking his SUV since it has more room in the back for our stuff."

I'm not looking forward to this four-hour drive with him. We got into a heated argument this morning before school, all because he overheard me talking to Bri– another friend of mine– about Brent asking me out. Sure, he's from the team, but Jayden acts like I'm a child and I can't date. He's always been so overprotective. I didn't say yes... but I also didn't say no either. I told Bri I was considering it since I haven't dated anyone for a long time and Brent seems like a nice guy, so I don't see what Jayden's problem is.

"Well..." she says, hesitating a bit, "...I hope you guys have a safe trip," she moves around the open door and wraps her arms around my neck. Wrapping my free arm around her waist, I hug her quickly.

"You too," I whisper. We hear raucous voices in the distance as we pull out of the quick hug. I don't have to look, knowing it's the football team coming out of practice. Glancing over my shoulder again and then back to Kenzi, she's blushing slightly, making me chuckle.

"I better get going before the guys get here," she says, and we laugh. "Talk to you soon. Have fun in the mountains," she smirks, waggling her eyebrows.

Rolling my eyes, I step back as she climbs into the front seat. "Oh yeah. Me, Jayden, and our parents. Soooooo much fun," I reply sarcastically. "Call me when you land in Texas, bitch."

Kenzi laughs at my response. "I will. Talk to you tomorrow, slut." Many people, our parents included, don't like our little nicknames for one another. It may be derogatory, but we feel that comfortable with each other that they have now become a constant term of endearment.

She closes the door, giving me a little wave as she starts her car. Backing away a bit, I watch as she puts it in reverse, backing out of the parking space. Watching as she slowly drives away, I can hear the footsteps and voices getting louder.

Walking to where Jayden parks his blood-red Acura MDX, I don't pay them any attention. They already get enough of that from all the other students around here, especially the girls. I am now wishing I would have driven myself today, especially with the argument Jayden and I got into over Brent.

"Sky," I hear Jayden's deep voice call. Continuing to walk, I ignore him since I don't want to argue with him in front of his buddies, nor do I want to deal with the shitty attitude that he usually has after a grueling practice. I hate fighting with him, and I know this will lead to possibly a bigger fight, but I just don't want it to happen now. I didn't see who was with him, and if Brent is there, it could lead to problems for him.

Laughter erupts from the others, which I know infuriates him. He hates being ignored, but he hates being laughed at even more. I feel the hair on the back of my neck stand on end, as if I can feel his glare all the way here. "Skylan," he barks louder as I reach his SUV. Moving to the other side of his car, I lean against the back passenger door. Hearing his footsteps quicken, I look down at the books in my hands and the bag resting on my shoulder feels even heavier.

Instead of unlocking the doors as usual, he walks around the vehicle to where I am, leaving his friends where they stand on the other side. Dropping his equipment bag with a loud thump onto the asphalt of the parking lot, he storms right up to me glaring, as I already knew he was. "I know you fucking heard me," he growls out in his deep baritone voice as he continues to glower down at me. "Why are you ignoring me?" he asks. With nowhere else to go, I cautiously look up into his reddened face. He's tall, towering over me at six foot three inches to my smaller five foot five frame. My books, firmly held against my chest, are the only thing standing between us.

Looking into his narrowed eyes, a soft gasp escapes my lips from the look on his face. He's furious. "Answer me, Sky.

Why didn't you fucking respond?" his voice a deep growl that only I can hear.

I barely register his friends on the other side of the vehicle now, because they are all quiet, trying to act like they aren't listening to our interaction. Maybe they are, maybe they aren't. It could just be them trying to not anger him any further. Jayden's anger is one of legends. Unlike his best friend Kyler, Jayden has anger issues that result in outbursts. Kyler's anger is silent but still as lethal. You won't see him coming until it's too late.

"Because I didn't want to deal with your attitude," I snap. We both stand there glaring at one another. His eyes narrow even further, almost as if he's trying to see into my mind to know exactly what I'm thinking. And trust me, he doesn't want to see what I'm thinking right now.

Jayden can sometimes be overbearing and very protective, but I know his heart is in the right place. He just wants to look out for me, which for the most part is sweet. It's always the way he goes about it. Protecting me shouldn't mean keeping me locked up away from everyone and everything.

My stepbrother is hot as hell, and I would probably be very attracted to him in another life or a different situation. Hell, I am attracted to him, with his tall and toned body with golden brown eyes and light brown hair that seems to always look like he just woke up. But our parents have always thrown us together as siblings, so I know he has never looked at me like that, nor will he ever. He looks at me like the bratty little sister he has to always watch out for and protect.

Exhaling a heavy breath and shaking his head, he reaches into his pocket for his keys. The high-pitch beeping is heard when he unlocks the doors. Neither of us break eye contact for what feels like several minutes, yet it was probably only a few seconds. Noticing the voices from his teammates have stopped, Jayden and I break eye contact. Closing his eyes for just a moment and taking a deep breath, he releases another heavy sigh.

"Just get in the damn car," he demands. His voice is rough yet resigned, but his eyes are still hard. Almost like there was more he wanted to say, but he held his tongue. I turn to open the door, but he grabs it first and yanks it open. Climbing into the passenger seat, I place my bag on the floorboard at my feet, placing my books in my lap. I stare forward, ignoring his steely gaze, watching me like he's expecting me to say more. He gives a slight shake of his head, then he closes the door.

From the corner of my eye, I see Jayden still staring at me before finally picking up his bag. He opens the door behind me and throws his bag into the seat, slamming the door closed so abruptly that the car physically shakes. He walks around the back of the vehicle to where his friends are all still standing quietly, talking among themselves.

Releasing a breath, I bend down, pulling my phone from my bag on the floor. This is going to be a very long and uncomfortable drive. Jayden is very unpredictable. He will either force me to talk about it or he will ignore me the whole way, causing me to find something to occupy myself for the entire trip. With that thought in mind, I type a message out to Bri.

2

JAYDEN

Continuing to shake my head as I round the back of my SUV, I walk to where my friends are standing. Skylan fucking infuriates me. I don't think she even realizes how much she affects me. Our parents have been married now for well over ten years, during that time, Skylan and I have become a lot closer than I initially expected we would. We spend so much time together that if I'm being honest, it was inevitable.

In the beginning, I was forced to hang out with her. My dad tried to make us into this perfect family. At first, I was so rebellious and tried anything and everything not to be around the brat. Being two years older than her also didn't help. However, the more time I spent with her, the more I saw her. The real her. The one she thinks no one else sees or notices, but I do. And I always have.

My step-sister is exotically beautiful with her golden skin and chestnut-colored hair. Hair that she can barely tame on a good day. With curves that she tries to hide, but it is absolutely impossible. And the girl is smart. Too smart for her own good. Skylan is noticed everywhere she goes, but she is so clueless about her beauty and attraction. She's asked me in the past why I am such an asshole when my friends come around. Shrugging, I usually don't answer her or tell her I don't want her around. But that couldn't be further from the truth. I've seen how my friends look at her, and trying to push down my attraction for her is hard enough. And now that asshole Brent thinks it's okay to go behind my back and ask her out. But Kyler and I have something in store for him.

"So what's the plan?" Thomas asks me as I walk up to where they are all standing. My teammates whisper amongst themselves but quiet down as I stop beside them. Shoving my hands in the pockets of my hoodie, I look around the guys standing there. Most of the team has already left. Only a few hung back.

Shrugging as I look at Thomas, I say, "I guess it's just me, you, Kyler, and Sky heading up to the cabin with my parents. Unless you guys want to go?" I ask the other three standing there. But I know they all have plans for the holiday. Bringing anyone else along would fuck up the entire plan Kyler and I have had in place for a couple of weeks now and would piss my best friend off severely. I'm sure getting Thomas to go along with it will be easy enough, but I can't take a chance with anyone else. It was difficult enough getting Ky to agree to bring Thomas in on this.

Glancing around at one another, they shake their heads.

"Can't. I'm flying home in the morning," Shane replies.

"Michael and I are heading home tomorrow afternoon. Our sister is coming home from Italy this weekend," Matthew says, talking about his twin brother and older sister. Both Matthew and Michael are on the team, but Michael's girlfriend came to practice, so he's probably with her right now. Nodding at him, I turn to look at Derek.

"Nah... I gotta drive to Savannah tonight," Derek says, adjusting his bag over his shoulder.

As each of my teammates gives their excuses, I nod. I try to look disappointed, but inside, I'm relieved. Glancing around the parking lot, I notice Kyler is missing, so I look at Thomas. "Where's Ky?" I ask, sounding exasperated. He glances around and shrugs, turning to chat with Derek standing next to him. Simultaneously, I glance down and reach into my pocket for my phone. Swiping to unlock it, I begin typing a message.

> Me: Where r u?

I stare at my phone for only a few seconds and see that he read the message. The three little dots bounce on the screen, and a new message pops up.

> Kyler: Had to go back to my place to finish packing. When are we leaving?

> Me: As soon as we grab our shit. Be there in 30

> Kyler: K

Looking around at our friends as I stuff my phone back in my pocket, I extend my fist. "Well, we have a four-hour trip tonight, so we gotta head out," I say, fist-bumping Shane first, then the others. Glancing at Thomas, I say, "Follow me to my house so you can leave your car there." Thomas nods and heads to his car after giving his fist bumps and playful punches.

As all the guys begin to head in different directions to each of their vehicles, I walk to the front driver's side of my

SUV. Before grabbing the handle, I glance in the driver's side window and see Skylan tapping away on her phone. My brows tighten at the sight before I open the door and climb in.

Looking over at her just before I push the start button, she stubbornly ignores me as I pull out of the parking spot. Once I see Thomas behind me, we head to our house.

Skylan and I live at home with our parents, but they are gone more than they are at home. Both have high-paying jobs that occupy their time and keep them traveling throughout the year. So it's basically like having a house on our own.

About five minutes into the drive, I glance over and see she is still typing away. Unable to see her screen, I wonder who it is she's furiously typing messages to. Probably Kenzi or Bri. At least it better be one of them and not that asshole Brent.

When I told Kyler about that motherfucker asking her out, he wanted to rip his head off his shoulders. He went feral in practice today. Every chance Kyler got, he targeted Brent with tackles and what Coach called, 'unnecessary roughness'. It was necessary to us. Brent is probably sporting a few more bruised ribs than necessary because of my best friend, and all I could do was sit back and laugh.

I shake my head at my inner thoughts. It drives me crazy to think of her talking to another guy. After this trip, I won't have to worry about that any longer. She will see who she belongs to and who will make sure she's taken care of in every way necessary.

With my eyes on the road but my thoughts on the brunette beauty sitting next to me, the excitement for this trip makes me want to vibrate out of my skin. Skylan tosses her hair over her shoulder, sending the smell of her jasmine shampoo to invade my senses even more than it already is. The thoughts, along with the scent, make my cock swell.

"Are you planning on ignoring me this entire trip?" I ask, leaning back in my seat and glancing over at her. My fist tightens on the steering wheel. Looking at me out of the corner of her eye but she still doesn't reply. "Seriously, Sky. What the fuck is going on?" I ask her.

Releasing a quick, harsh breath, I hear her lock her phone as she stuffs it between her thighs. I glance down at the phone, then back to her eyes quickly before focusing on the road again. Fuck, how I would love to have my hand there as we're driving.

"I'm tired of you treating me like a child, Jay," she says matter-of-factly as she angles herself slightly to face me.

I have always admired how Skylan can speak her mind. That's why it always frustrates me when she ignores or avoids me, but this response confuses me, and I show it on my face.

"What the hell are you going on about? I don't treat you like a child," I respond, probably a little too harshly, but it's what she expects from me also.

"Yes, you do, Jay," she says, softening her voice and leaning her head against the headrest. "You may not realize it, but you do."

Silence settles inside the car, but after a few moments, I look over and see how sad her eyes look. Releasing a breath and all my anger from earlier, I glance at her. I notice she is staring in my direction but not looking at my face. Her gaze is far off, and her face looks forlorn. Reaching across the console, I grasp her chin gently with my thumb and fore-finger until her eyes focus on mine. With only glances at the slick road, I focus on her, letting her know she has my full attention.

"I'm sorry," I say quietly. She stares at me for a minute without a reply, so I continue. "It's not that I'm treating you like a child, Sweetness. I worry about you, is all." A small smile creeps over my lips, one that no one ever sees but her. I wish she understood. Wish she comprehended how much I care about her and what lengths I would go to make her happy and keep her safe.

I can tell my words finally relax her a bit because she nods and gives me a small smile of her own. "Okay," she breathes almost inaudibly. I give her chin a playful little shake, but I don't remove my hand. The opportunity to touch her has been so far and few between that I take advantage when I can. Chuckling, she slowly reaches up to grasp the wrist holding her face. I feel tingles along my skin, and once again, like every other time when I'm around her, my cock starts to stir. Fuck, this girl is beautiful. Inside and out.

As I look away from the road again, my eyes glance between her dark chocolate eyes and pouty lips, then back again. My thumb slowly moves over her chin, letting the tip barely graze her bottom lip. It could be construed as an accident, but I know differently. I want to know what those lips feel like on my own. What they taste like. What they feel like wrapped about my cock.

Her lips part with a small gasp at the electric touch. She doesn't move from my hold, but her hand tightens on my wrist. It feels like she's about to pull my hand away, but she doesn't. The air in the car is thick with sexual tension, and I don't know how I'm going to hold back from touching her for the entire ride. Especially knowing how close we are to making all of our desires a reality. This is where I usually leave and stay with Kyler to escape from her for a bit.

Smiling again, I drop my hand to the gear shift between

us. Clearing my throat because I know if I didn't, my voice would be huskier than usual with lust. This girl is doing all sorts of things to my head and body. "Are you finished packing?" I ask instead of addressing the elephant in the room or the car.

Releasing a heavy breath, she sounds almost as if she is disappointed by the turn of events. "Yeah. I have everything ready. Just need to load it into the back. What about you?" She says, looking over at me.

"My stuff is already loaded in the back," I say, motioning over my shoulder. "I just need to drop my equipment bag off."

Nodding, she turns her attention to watch the passing trees and traffic. As we continue to our house, I glance over at her several times. She looks deep in thought. Usually, Sky would be on her phone or playing with the radio, trying to find a song she likes, but she bites her bottom lip as she stares out the side window. What I wouldn't give to bite that bottom lip of hers myself. *Just a little while longer*, I keep reminding myself.

We pull into our driveway and slow to a stop just in front of the house. Still deep in thought and without speaking, Skylan reaches for the door handle. Grabbing her arm, not harshly but enough to capture her attention, she looks back at me, a little shocked. "Are we... are we okay?" I ask her.

Giving me a small smile, she nods her head. "Yeah. We're okay," she answers softly. We stare at one another until her door is pulled open, breaking the connection. Jumping back slightly and gasping, she looks at who opened her door. I guess she didn't realize Thomas was behind us the whole way.

"You guys coming?" Thomas innocently asks with a

giant goofy smile, making me laugh. Skylan's head whips back in my direction with a look of confusion.

"Oh yeah," I said, grabbing the door handle and giving her a devious smirk. "I forgot to tell you. Your mom and my dad said that Thomas and Kyler could come since their parents were out of the country and had nowhere to go for the holiday," I say, shrugging, opening the door, and stepping out.

Keeping Skylan in the dark was part of the plan. We didn't want her to know much until the last minute. She thinks our parents are driving in tomorrow; however, they aren't expected for a few days, which is part of our well-laid-out plan. The only part we haven't wholly secured is Thomas. But I know he'll be on board. I've seen the way he looks at her.

Before closing the driver's side door, I hear Sky release a deep sigh. She looks back at Thomas, and when she speaks, I can hear the smile in her voice. "Well, I'm glad you're coming. Maybe with you there, someone will actually hang out with me." Hearing the sarcasm in her words being thrown my way, I chuckle and slam my door shut.

Sky and Thomas have always been somewhat friends. He always went out of his way to talk to her and ensure she was safe and comfortable whenever I was not around. They have a few classes together, so he makes sure people leave her alone. I know that he likes her more than he lets on, but he won't do anything because she's my stepsister, and he won't cross that line. But that will change during this trip.

"Absolutely, Butterfly. We have two weeks to watch movies, play cards, eat junk food, or whatever you want," I hear Thomas say, throwing his arm over her shoulders in a casual way. Rounding the back of my SUV, I see them walking toward the front door.

"Dude," I growl out, capturing his attention as I yank open the back door to retrieve my equipment bag. Laughing as he looks over his shoulder at me, I glare at him from over the door. "Go put your shit in the back of my car and drive around to the garage. You can park in my spot," I say.

Leaning down, Thomas kisses Skylan on the top of her head. As he walks past me, giving me a sly smirk, I shoot him a vicious glare. "Asshole," I hiss at him. Grabbing my equipment bag, I slam the door closed. I can hear Thomas laugh as he opens the door to his car to grab his stuff.

3

JAYDEN

"Damn, dude. This place is huge," Thomas says from the backseat. After stopping at the store a few miles down the main road to grab food, drinks, and junk food, we pull into the gravel driveway to our family cabin. Thomas leans forward between the front seats, his mouth agape and eyes wide. Our cabin is very secluded in the mountains between Pigeon Forge and Gatlinburg. It's a beautiful view up here to the Great Smokey Mountains and a small escape from city life. Our parents like it up here, away from everything and everyone.

I remember when we were younger, Skylan and I used to go hiking together all the time. It was during those times we became so close. Discovering each other's dreams and fears, discussing what we wanted out of life. As time went on, it was all about delving further and further into her head so that I could become the person she could seek out and look to. The person she could grow to love as more than the brother that was forced on her.

I park in the little open garage at the front, and we all climb out. "Let's get everything inside, and then I can show you around," I say. Heading to the back of my SUV, we begin to unload the groceries and luggage. It takes a few trips to bring it all inside the house.

Once we have all the groceries in the kitchen, we start to bring our luggage upstairs. "Our parents' room is the master suite downstairs. Mine and Sky's rooms are up here, and the guest rooms are up here, too," I say, climbing the stairs.

"Rooms?" Thomas asks. "As in plural?" he questions, making Kyler roll his eyes. Kyler has been here once before. Last year, we came here with Shane and Derek for a guy's getaway. Plus, his family is as wealthy as ours, so he's used to the extravagance of summer and winter homes.

"Yeah. This is a five-bedroom cabin. So you both get your own room," Skylan says, smiling as we reach the top landing before heading to the left toward her room. We all watch her pulling her bag behind her until she closes the door behind her. Once I hear her door click shut, I turn and look at the guys. Chuckling, I notice they are still looking in the direction she disappeared to.

I gesture to where she's just gone, down the dark wood hallway with sparse photos of holidays and trips of the past. Pictures of Skylan and I skiing, hiking, and roughhousing in the cabin's front yard. "That way is mine and Sky's rooms." I drop my bags on the landing before heading to the right of the stairs, where there are two other bedrooms and a bathroom.

This hallway is the same as ours, except with a separate bathroom, where Sky and I share a connecting bathroom. This hallway has photos of the family and friends that have been here in the years past. Thomas and Kyler follow close behind me. I open the first door on the right, and Kyler walks right in. The room is open and large, with dark blue walls and a queen-sized bed in the middle of the room. The comforter on the bed is a shade lighter than the walls, and the room smells like freshly laundered clothes.

He heads directly to the bed and tosses his bags down on it. Immediately, Kyler unzips his bag and starts pulling things out. "I guess Ky is claiming this one," I say with a laugh. Thomas peeks his head into the room and looks around. His eyes still widened with wonderment.

"Come on. I will show you the other room," I say. I point to the door across the hallway from Kyler's room. "That's the bathroom you guys will share. And this..." I say, opening the door at the end of the hall. "...is your room."

Thomas walks through the door, dropping his stuff on the dark hardwood floor just inside. "Damn, Jay. This is nicer than my room at home," he says with a smile, walking through the room and looking in every direction, trying to take everything in. Sitting on the bed, he lets his hands roam over the beige comforter that is laid out on the queen-sized bed. The walls in this room are a dark chocolate that matches the floors. My parents have all dark colors throughout the cabin, even in my room. The only room that has lighter colors is Skylan's. Her room has all shades of pink.

"Closet is just there," I say, pointing at the only other door in the room. "Make yourself comfortable, and we will meet downstairs in a bit after everyone gets settled in," I say as I walk to the door.

"Cool," he says absentmindedly, still looking around the room. I go to close the door behind me, and I hear Thomas call my name.

"Yeah," I say, sticking my head back inside the door to look at him.

"Thanks. You know... for inviting me to stay with you guys."

Nodding, I give him a crooked smile. "Of course. What are friends for, my dude?" I say, closing the door behind me.

Standing outside his door, I wonder how all this will work. I try to think of every outcome that could happen after we tell him. Thomas likes Skylan, but how will he feel about our idea before revealing ourselves? If he disagrees, he could throw a wrench in our plans before they even start. I can't allow anything to come between me and her, and I know with Kyler's temper, he definitely will lose his shit. As unpredictable as Kyler is, he could end up beating the shit out of Thomas. I have to figure out the best way to explain our intentions and reasons to get him on board.

Making my way to the other side, where Sky's and my rooms are, I grab my stuff from where I dropped it at the top of the stairs. Entering my room, I drop my bags on my bed on top of the black and red comforter. My entire room is black, dark red, and gray. The walls are dark gray with a black border along the top and bottom. A tall black armoire sits in the corner next to the red settee, and a long black dresser is against the far wall by my desk with a red and black gaming chair. I rarely spend time here, but I want to feel comfortable when I do.

Thinking about Skylan next door and what Kyler and I have planned, I run through all the scenarios and the 'what ifs'. We've had this planned for a few months now. Bringing Thomas along may have complicated things, but we will have to see. Things could go very wrong, or they could go very right. This holiday is about to be very hard... in more ways than one. Unzipping my bag, I shake my head and begin to unpack.

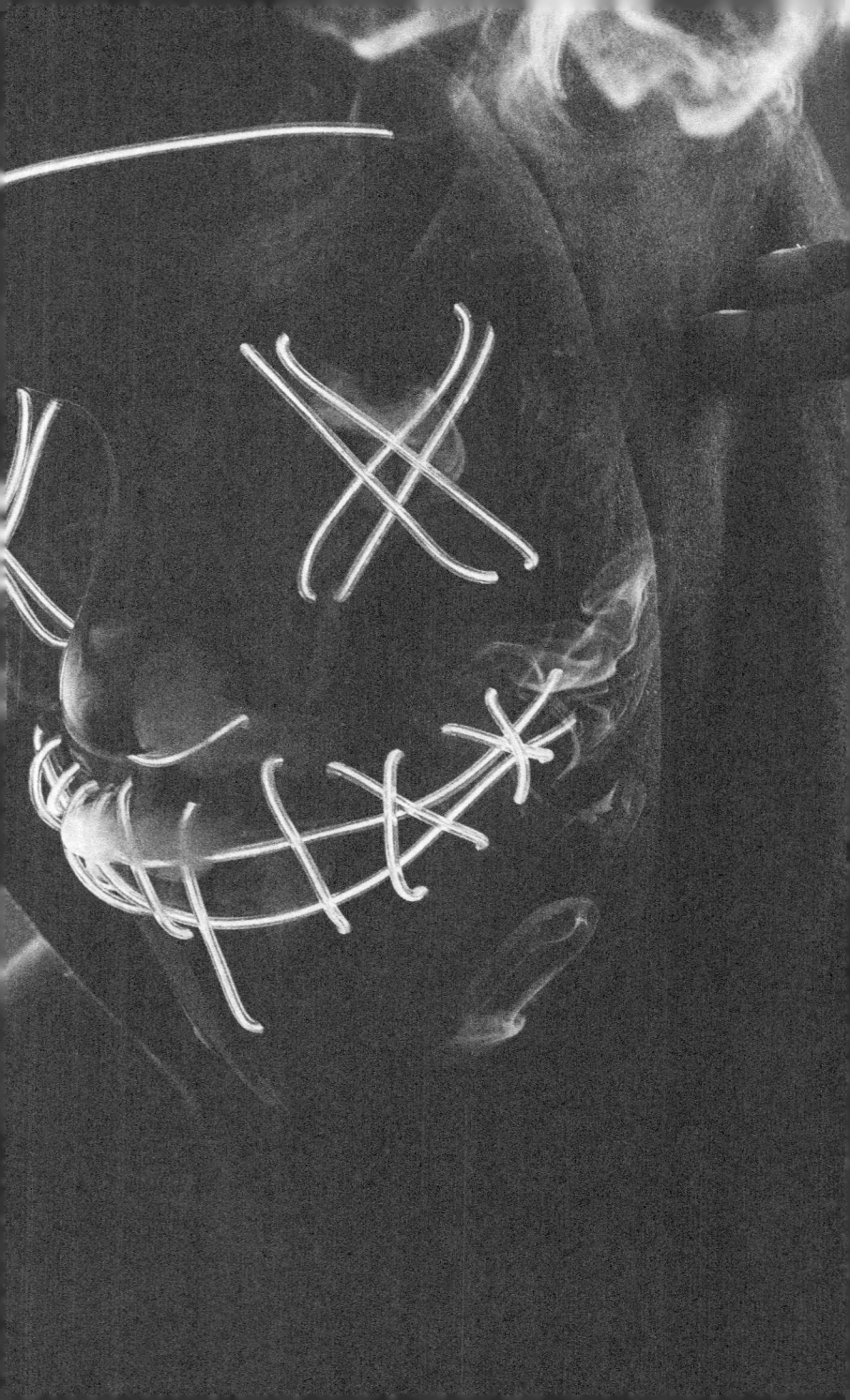

4

KYLER

As I lie on the bed with my hands behind my head, I stare at the ceiling. I was hoping that jerking off back at my place would ease my insatiable need for her, but it's done nothing to curb the feeling. Sitting in that car for the last four and half hours, smelling her jasmine scent as it enveloped me and causing me to stay hard the entire time, didn't help. This girl has no idea what she does to me.

Watching her joke around with Thomas and Jayden makes my blood boil. I wish I could be that casual with her and that I didn't get infuriatingly jealous every single damn time. But it's crazy because I'm not jealous knowing the plans that I have to share her with my best friend or friends if Thomas is in on this, but I'm envious as hell that she doesn't look at me the way she does them.

When Jayden saw it in my eyes, he almost beat my ass. Especially when he already knows my proclivities and needs during sex. It took a while to explain to him exactly how I feel about her, and the fact that it's not only sexual or the physical attraction, but also the inclination to protect and take care of her. Granted, there is still the hunger. The need. Her body calls to my most primal nature in every way.

It's only been the last year or so that I've noticed Skylan since Jay and I have been friends. I never looked at her that way until recently because she's his sister. Or stepsister, as he constantly reminds me. No blood relation. He emphasizes that, seeing as he has the same feelings about her. We've discussed this in length.

At first, it was just us fantasizing and comparing her to every girl we've been with. But then, Jayden found her journal and read it. We knew it was a violation of her privacy, but at the time, he was desperate to see inside her head in any way possible. The things she divulged there were so descriptive and on par with my darkness that I just couldn't let this opportunity pass without trying something. So when this holiday came up, we discussed how if we made some of her darkest fantasies come true, maybe that would be our in. We decided then that we would not make her choose after we reveal ourselves to her. That jealousy would not be part of this equation, and our only goal was to ensure she was happy and cared for.

Sitting up on the bed, I look out the large bay window into the woods. The snow is starting to fall. Enough to coat the ground, but not heavy enough to cause worry. Standing from the bed, I walk to the window, place my hands on the ledge, and look up at the darkening sky. Clouds are coating it, where no stars can be seen, making this area even darker. We are far enough up the mountains that no city lights pollute the night sky. Seeing anything standing right before you is almost impossible when it gets dark up here.

Lowering my eyes to the woods outside of my window makes me smile. I can imagine myself chasing her there. I can almost hear her panting and heavy breathing as she runs from me, knowing I will catch her and what I will do to her when I do. My cock stiffens just thinking about pushing her up against a tree and how she will struggle against me. Begging me to stop, all the while, her body is screaming for me to continue. I can almost feel her short nails scratching down my arms and back, but she won't realize that the pain and fight fuel my lustful hunger for her.

Losing track of time, I daydream about Skylan and what I want to do to her tight, curvaceous body until I hear a knock on the door. "Yeah," I call out, glancing over my shoulder.

The door opens, and Jayden walks in, closing the door quietly behind him. He walks inside, and I turn to look back out the window again.

"You okay?" he asks me. "You barely said two words on the ride here."

I look back over my shoulder at him, glowering. "What the fuck do you think?" I say and turn to face him. My head is spinning with thoughts of her still. It doesn't help that I can still smell her jasmine scent on my clothes. Crossing my arms over my muscular chest, I lean against the wooden window sill. I'm still angry that he felt like he needed to bring Thomas with us. This wasn't the plan, and I hate improvisation.

"I think we're close to getting what we want. That's what I think," Jayden says as he walks over to the oversized plush chair in the corner of the room. Throwing himself back into the chair, he crosses his leg over his other knee and stretches his arms out over the armrests.

We've all grown close since Jayden came to Georgia Tech. All three of us are on the football team and have some sort of computer major, and while Thomas is a friend and teammate, Jayden and I are closer. We do almost everything together.

After a few minutes of silence and Jayden staring at me, I push off the sill, walk over to the bed where I still have my open duffle bag, and begin unpacking things, throwing them into the drawers.

"Have you told Thomas?" I grunt out as I shove some clothes haphazardly into the top drawer. I wonder how he thinks we're getting close to what we want when we literally could have brought the largest cockblock with us.

"Not yet. I wanted to make sure she wouldn't overhear us. I know she's gonna be taking a shower soon. We'll wait until then," he responds. Thoughts of her in the shower unbiddenly race through my mind—her naked and wet, soaping herself up. Shaking my head to rid myself of the mental image, I keep moving.

"Fine," I say gruffly. "But you better hope he goes for it," I say, glancing over at him.

Smiling at me, he stands up from the chair. He stretches and groans out loud. "Oh, I know he will. Thomas has had a thing for Sky since he met her. He will do anything for a chance with her," he says as he walks to the door. After opening it, he looks back at me. "Trust me, Ky. Thomas is just as hungry as we are. He's just better at hiding it."

He better hope he's right. I'm not letting anything get in my way any longer. I've waited too long. Staring at one another, I give him a stern nod. "With or without Thomas... I'm making Skylan James mine."

A sinister smile envelopes Jayden's face. "Ours, Kylan," he replies. "She is ours." I watch as he leaves my room and closes the door behind himself. Staring at the door just a bit longer, I really hope he's right.

5

JAYDEN

Walking up to Skylan's door, I hesitate momentarily before knocking. I hear her sweet voice calling from inside, telling me to come in. Turning the knob, I step inside to see her putting her clothes away. We haven't even been here an hour, and the room is saturated in her smell. She walks back and forth between her suitcase on the bed and closet. Walking over, I sit down on her soft bed.

"You okay?" I ask as I lean back on my elbows, stretching my legs out in front of me. She continues to move around her room, yet my eyes don't leave her as she does. Every move she makes is fluid and hypnotizing.

"Yeah. Just a little tired from the drive," she replies with a smile. "What about you? Aren't you tired?" she says as she glances at me and moves to place the items in her hands in the dresser. Looking at me over her shoulder, she stands directly in front of me. Fuck, she is perfect for me. For us. She just doesn't know it yet. But we will show her, and she will see soon enough. I know my dad is going to want my head for pursuing her like this, but I don't care. I have held off long enough. Because he also taught me to take what I want, and I want her. He also taught me if anything is worth having, it's worth fighting for, and I'm about to put that to the test.

"Just a little. But I'm gonna hang with the guys for a bit. Why don't you take a shower? We can make something to eat after you're out," I say, moving to stand up, but she doesn't push back. We're standing so close I can smell her. Looking down into her dark brown eyes, I take another step closer. It's taking the pure will of strength not just to lean down and kiss her right now, especially when she looks at me like that.

"Okay," she whispers, and I smile down at her. Smiling with her and because of her is so easy. Effortless actually. Just being in her presence calms me. At least most times. Sometimes, she can push all my buttons.

"Take your time, sweetness. We're in no rush," I whisper and move past her to leave. If I don't move now, I'm not sure I could hold myself back any longer. We're so close. I just need to hold on a little longer.

Walking through her door, I pull it closed with a quiet snick. I stand outside the wooden barrier for a few more minutes until I hear the shower turn on. Closing my eyes momentarily, I lean on her wood door with my hand. I know making her mine... ours... is the right thing, but I'm really hoping the way we do this doesn't destroy our relationship in the process. Hearing the glass door to the shower close, I head to Thomas's room.

I knock on Thomas' door and turn the knob at the same time, walking in. Thomas pops his head out of the closet with a look of confusion until he sees me, and then a smile crosses his face. "Hey bro, what's up?" he asks before returning to the closet and finishing hanging up his clothes.

Sitting on the bed, I lean forward with my elbows resting

on my knees, looking down at the ground. There is silence until Thomas slowly exits the closet with a look of concern on his face. As he walks closer, I finally look up at him. He just stands there looking down at me. "We need to talk," I say, motioning with my head for him to sit beside me on the bed.

Slowly, he moves to sit down next to me. Nervous energy surrounds him, and it is practically suffocating me. "Jay... what's wrong?" he asks.

"Look, T. I want you to know I'm glad you're here. Hell, we all are. But I need you to know..." I say and sigh deeply, looking back down at the floor. Shaking my head slowly, I try to think how I will explain what this holiday is supposed to consist of.

The uncomfortable silence finally gets to Thomas, so he huffs out a breath. "Just spit it out already, Jay," he says as he leans down, mimicking my stature.

Rubbing the bridge of my nose with my fingers, I try to think of the best way to say it. "Let me ask you a question," I cautiously say. Looking over at him with seriousness, I hope he feels the same way, and by the look in his eyes, he does. "What type of feelings do you have for Skylan?" I ask with my brow furrowed, looking directly into his eyes. He knows I don't play when it comes to her.

The shock of my question shows on his face and in his eyes. His mouth opens and closes like a fish out of water. I want to laugh at his reaction, but I don't. Keeping a straight face, I wait for him to answer. His eyes never waiver, but I see the fear creep into them.

"Wh... what do you... wh-what do you mean, Jay? I don't have feelings for Sky," he stutters, making me glare at him. "I mean, besides being her friend, that is."

"Don't treat me like I'm stupid, T. I've seen how you look

at her. And how you act whenever she comes around. Now answer my damn question," I demand a little more harsher than I intended. But I need him to admit it before we go any further.

His eyes dance between mine, trying to gauge how I will react, I'm sure. I continue to hold his gaze without wavering. After an uncomfortable silence, I raise my eyebrow, silently questioning him again. I can tell when he finally decides just to come clean. I can see the resolve in his eyes as he releases a heavy breath.

"I've liked Skylan for a long time, Jay. I care about her more than I should, but I would never go there out of respect for you and our friendship. But that's why I keep her as a friend if she needs anything. I'm there," he quickly replies. I'm sure he feels saying it fast is like pulling off the proverbial bandaid. The quicker, the better. I sit there and just stare at him. "But I swear, Jay, I wouldn't try anything with her."

He's getting more nervous the longer I stare at him. "Why not?" I question with a deep growl.

He sits there, still staring at me. Confusion is written all over his face. "She... she's your sister," he replies hesitantly, his brows furrowing at the question. A devious smirk crosses my face, which I know he probably feels is more sinister. Thomas has seen me when I've lost control but never once lost my cool.

"She's my step sister. Not blood-related. You do know that, right?" I ask him, and his head slowly nods. He still doesn't speak. I can tell it's because he doesn't want to say anything wrong, especially about Sky. He was there the day I almost killed Aaron. I probably would have if Kyler hadn't pulled me off of him. He was running his fucking mouth, telling everyone how he was going to get Skylan drunk at the frat party and fuck her. Over my dead body. Or his. Aaron doesn't even realize that Kyler saved his life that night. Even though Kyler wished it was him that broke that fuckers jaw, not me. I almost got suspended from the team over that fight. Luckily, several players were there and overheard what he was saying, so he was the one in trouble with the university.

"Okay, T. What if I told you that you could have a chance with her? Would you take it?" I ask him. The silence after this question is deafening, but I won't be the one to break it this time.

"Is this a trick question?" he replies, his question making me chuckle.

"No, it's not. Just answer the damn question," I say. He studies my eyes, looking so long, I wonder if he will answer me.

"Of course, I would. I told you... I have cared for Skylan for a long time. Since I met her," he says, letting a harsh breath go. I can tell he is nervous about me hitting him or something else along those lines. The hesitancy in his words speaks volumes about his respect and reluctance to lose our friendship. But that's not what this is about. This is more so about us building on our friendship.

Nodding my head, I look back down at the floor. Clasping my hands, I consider my following words seriously. "Okay..." I say, rubbing my face with both hands roughly. "...we're friends, T. So I trust that whatever I say, and whatever happens here in this cabin, stays with us, right?" I ask, finally looking over at him.

He tilts his head with his brow furrowed. "Of course, Jay. I would never betray your confidence. Like... ever," he exhales, both of us still staring at each other. "What is it, Jayden? What's going on?" he asks me quietly.

Releasing a heavy breath, I just decide to come out with it. We're all here now. Kyler and I have been discussing this trip for months, and we both know nothing will stop this. "How would you feel about..." I hesitate, nibbling on my bottom lip. This is the hardest part. Explaining how Kyler and I feel about her and what we have planned for her. "... sharing her?" After speaking the last words, I hold my breath, waiting on pins and needles for his reaction and response. The air is electric, and all my nerves are on edge.

His face holds moments of confusion, and then his eyes widen as the words I just said settle on him. My heart is pounding, waiting to hear his answer.

"Share? Like... with you?" he asks, sitting up straight, staring incredulously at me. "But... she's your... um, sister." Before I can even open my mouth, he starts waving his hands in front of himself trying to stave off my argument before I can say anything. "Yeah, yeah... I know. She's not blood-related. But I didn't think you liked her like that. I mean, I've seen you be protective of her, but I always thought it was because she was your sister."

Nodding at his words, I give a light shrug of my shoulders. "Yes... and no. In the beginning, when we were younger, yes. It was because she was my stepsister, and my dad tried very hard for us to act like a family," I say and again look down at the floor. I take a deep breath because Kyler is the only other one I've ever confided this in. I squeeze my eyes closed and shake my head slowly.

I feel Thomas nudge my leg with his. "It's okay, Jay. You can trust me. I swear what is said here stays here," he quietly says, making me glance up at him and give him a small smile.

Nodding, I try to continue. "Well... somewhere along the way, my feelings changed. I don't even know how to describe them. Her presence takes over my thoughts constantly," I say. Chuckling, I shake my head. "T... I can't even fuck another chick without thinking about it being her."

"So what do you want to do?" he asks me, still unsure about what is happening here. But that's okay because I know what needs to happen.

"That's a complicated answer," I say and look at him just as there is a knock on his door. Glancing at the door, then back at Thomas, wondering if he will answer it. Raising an eyebrow, he stares at me for a few more minutes.

"Yeah," he calls out before finally looking away from me and to the door.

The door slowly opens, and Kyler stalks in. Eyeing me with a scowl on his face, he closes the door with a quiet click. "Fuck," I say under my breath and drop my head. At the quiet word, Thomas's head whips back to look at me, then back to Kyler.

Kyler stuffs his hands inside his pockets, leaning against the wall beside the door. Looking up at him, he's staring at me with his usual glare. He's tired of waiting. Tired of the unknown that having Thomas here brings. But I understand the feeling, but we can't rush this now. Not with us so close to the end game. We've waited this long, so now we need to push forward. Thomas must be on board for this to play out how we want it.

Kyler and I stare at one another. As best friends and as close as we are, we can read each other better than anyone else. And I know he's asking if everything is going according to plan. He just stands there. His eyes jump quickly, looking at Thomas and then back to me. When I finally look at Thomas, I see his attention is also pulled between Kyler and me. The room is fraught with tension right now for different reasons.

Thomas jumps to his feet. "Okay. Someone, please tell me what the fuck is going on here," he says, looking between us. His sudden movement makes me sit up, but Kyler doesn't budge. Kyler's eyes bore holes into mine at this, knowing I have yet to fully explain to Thomas what is necessary.

"Fine," I say, resigned and leaning my elbows back on my knees. "We have been planning this holiday for quite a while now. Kyler and I both want Skylan, and our friendship is too strong to allow her to come between us. So..." I say, taking a deep breath and releasing it before continuing. "We've decided we're okay with sharing her as long as it's just us," I finish and look up into Thomas' eyes. "But I have known how you feel about her for a while, so we discussed it, and we are okay with you being part of this as well. As long as you're okay with it."

His mouth is opening and closing like a damn fish again. I think I shocked the hell out of him with all this information so quickly. He keeps glancing between Kyler and me. My best friend doesn't move or say anything. He's letting me run this show. Which is probably best, seeing as his way of discussing anything is either with his fists or by demanding compliance.

"You two are serious," he whispers, staring at me as I nod. He looks back at Kyler, who just stares at him with that unnerving straight face of his that will make any grown-ass man shit himself. I've been on the receiving end of that stare and am glad we're best friends.

Slowly, he moves back to the bed and drops down on it. He throws himself back to lie down, facing the ceiling with his hands covering his face. Everything we told him is a lot to take in, so I understand his need to soak it all in. I look at

Kyler, who raises an eyebrow at me. I give him a look, telling him to give Thomas time to process.

Thomas releases a deep breath in a huff, and with that, I can tell he's reached a conclusion. Slowly, he sits up, resting his elbows on his knees and focusing on the floor momentarily before his eyes zero in on me. I see his resolve; just as I predicted, he will do whatever it takes.

"What's the plan to get her on board with this?" he asks me. I give a small, devious smile as my eyes move over to Kyler, who just nods his approval with no change in his demeanor.

6

KYLER

S tanding here stoically, I sit and listen to Jayden explain our crazy-ass plan to Thomas. Every so often, he shakes his head with disbelief on his face and glances my way. Pulling my hands from my pockets, I cross my arms over my chest and my leg in front of the other. Thomas keeps looking at me as Jayden tells him my part in all of this, with what appears to me as fear. But I'm used to people being afraid of me. I know I can be considered scary.

I have particular tastes when it comes to sex, and this whole plan begins with me. I have known little Miss Skylan has had a crush on me for a while, but little does she know that the feelings are reciprocated. I have been so enamored with her that I have issues with fucking anyone that doesn't look like her. Now, I just don't know how to handle these crazy feelings. Plus the fact that, until recently, did I think she would be able to or even want to manage my proclivities toward sex.

After months of fighting it, I finally confided in my best friend. I took the chance to get it off my chest, hoping that talking to him about it would help. Maybe he would kick my ass for looking at his sister like that, or maybe getting it off my chest would allow me to see that I'm not suitable for her. That I will never be worthy of her goodness. Now I know that I am what she's looking for, and I'm going to give her every bit of darkness in me, hoping like hell she can withstand the depravity of what I bring.

Finding out that Jayden also feels the same about Skylan was a bit of a shock to me. He just doesn't have the propensity for the type of sex that I do. While discussing with him, we decided to allow me my opportunity to give her what she's been seeking and what I have been craving, and then... they can take part in the fun.

"So..." Thomas says as he scrubs his face with his hands, hesitating a minute and releasing a long breath. "...tell me if I have this right. Jayden and I will leave—"

"No," I say, interrupting him. "We are all technically leaving. At least that's what she will think." Thomas nods in understanding.

"Okay," he says, contemplating everything we told him during this entire conversation. Looking up at me this time, he holds my stare. "Yeah, okay. I'm in. I just hope this doesn't backfire on us," he grunts as Jayden's phone rings. Standing up, Jayden digs in his pocket to retrieve his phone.

He answers the phone after looking at the caller ID and then at me. "Hey, Dad," he says. That captures Thomas's attention. With all the talk of our plans, the thought of parental units had escaped us. Jayden stands and begins moving around the room with the phone pressed against his ear. Thomas and I watch him with rapt attention. Stopping, Jayden slowly turns to face us. His smile grows sinister as he listens and nods his head.

Dropping my arms to my side, I stand straight away from the wall. Jayden's eyes focus on me as he replies to his father, but his voice doesn't match the look on his face, and my brow furrows. "That sucks, Dad. I was looking forward to this vacation with you guys. I know Sky will be disappointed, too."

Taking a few steps away from the wall, a slight smirk graces my lips. Thomas quickly stands from the bed as well. This is too fucking good to be true. Here, we thought we would only have a few days with her. Now we have two whole fucking weeks.

"Yeah, we stopped and grabbed food and stuff on our way to the cabin. Me and the guys will make sure we're all stocked up," Jayden continues, speaking with his dad. Thomas and I glance at one another. This can't be happening. Things can't just fall together like this. "Alright. We'll call you in a couple of days," he says. "Love you, too," he responds to his dad, then ends the call and puts his phone back into his pocket.

"Seriously?" I question, with my brows raised. Jayden nods slowly with a devious smirk on his face. A smile slowly creeps up the side of my lips. A smile that I rarely wear. "Well..." I drawl out slowly, rubbing my hands together. "This vacation just got a little more interesting," I say, looking over to see Thomas smiling as well. "And not as rushed. We can take our time with this."

"Time to put this plan into action then, huh?" Jayden questions. Thomas nods, but I just look at Jay. He knows this has been a long time coming for me, so I don't acknowledge that question. Chills break out all over my skin with just the vision of chasing her. Holding her down and touching her is something I have dreamt of for so long. Her flesh laid bare to us to worship, taste... mark. Jayden centers his eyes on me. "Are you sure this is how you want to start this?" he questions me.

Slowly stalking forward with my brows furrowed deep, I step up toe to toe with Jayden, glaring at him. "We discussed this, Jay. Are you backing out?" I growl out. Jayden is slightly shorter than I am, and we are very close in stature. We both train hard at school for football and to keep our physique up to par.

Jayden doesn't move as I stand in front of him. "I didn't say that, Ky. I just need to make sure that you're ready if she freaks out on you," he says.

It's definitely not something that I haven't thought about. I know if this shot with her is blown, there is no second chance. But she's worth the chance because it's either this or leave her alone completely, and I don't think I have it in me to do that.

"If she does, you can swoop in and save the day. Be the big brother she always looks to for protection," I say, clapping him on the shoulder hard. "And I can continue being the asshole prick she thinks I am."

Jayden chuckles, looking up into my eyes.

"But I know..." I continue. "I fucking know she won't. She wants this as much as we do. So, let's do this."

We both look at Thomas, who is glancing between the two of us; he nods with a smile. "Let's do this," he repeats my words.

Jayden finally looks back at me, holding out his fist, which I bump with mine. "Yeah. Let's do this." I have this overwhelming feeling that this will be the best two weeks of our lives.

7

SKYLAN

As the door clicks shut, I stand staring at where Jayden just left, but I don't hear his footsteps move away. He's been acting strange lately. His ups and downs with me are so intense and infuriating. One minute, he's yelling about someone I've been talking to or somewhere I've been, and the next, he's being sweet and nice. It's confusing and very draining.

Looking at the small crack under the door, I can tell he's still standing just outside my room, waiting for me to get in the shower. Shaking my head, I walk into the adjoining bathroom between mine and his rooms and turn on the shower, allowing the water to heat up. I make sure that I close the glass door to the shower loud enough that he hears it, to make him think I'm in there already.

This bathroom is one thing I love about this cabin more than anything. It's so big, and while it's a bit rustic with the wood walls and ceiling, the modern tile floor and step-up walk-in shower are a dream. The shower is all glass with two little tile benches in each corner of the almost triangular-shaped area, with a showerhead like normal up above, but it also has four wallheads that face the center. Our parents spared no expense when they got this place and renovated it.

Walking back out to my room, I watch his feet slowly move from in front of my door, and I don't know whether to be relieved or disappointed. Shaking my head, I walk to my dresser to grab a pair of black spandex shorts and a t-shirt, with a clean sports bra and pink thong.

I move slowly back into the bathroom. Sitting the clothes on top of the dark brown fluffy towel I have laid out, I prop myself up on the cold counter with my back to the mirror as I grip the edge of the granite with both hands. I let my head settle back on my shoulders, looking up at the ceiling as I let crazy images run through my head. Knowing I'm under the same roof as three of the hottest Georgia Tech football players makes my fantasies and thoughts go haywire. Even if one of those players is my hot as sin step brother. I know I don't have a chance in hell with any of them, but I can't help but wonder what it would be like. To be their object of attention.

Yeah, yeah. I know I shouldn't lust after him or his friends. I know they are hands-off and way out of my league. But I can dream and wish, can't I? I chuckle at my own thoughts. Shaking my head, I look around the bathroom. The steam is building from the hot water cascading in the shower. The shower here is large enough for a party, which makes me smile. Thinking about what exactly can happen in that shower.

But just as quickly as the image forms, then the unbidden thoughts of Jayden and his friends coming up here for their guys' trip make my smile drop. I know they had girls in here doing whatever it is that they do. Jealousy and anger burn deep in my stomach. I hate the double standards. He's allowed to fuck around with whoever he wants, but god forbid I want just to date someone.

Shaking my head to rid myself of those thoughts, I push away from the counter and stand up. Wiping my hand across my brow, then through my unruly hair, I turn to look in the mirror. My body drips from the steam and humidity that is saturating the room now. I grab a hair tie from my little makeup bag on the counter so I can pull my hair up into a messy bun.

Slowly, I get undressed as I watch myself in the mirror until I'm standing completely naked. I stare at my reflection, wondering what the guys look for in a woman and what it is that I lack. Tilting my head back and forth, twisting slightly to look at myself from a few different angles, I try to see what they see when they look at me. I know I'm pretty by ordinary standards, but I've seen the girls hanging off Kyler, Thomas, and Jayden's arms after games and at the frat parties. They are gorgeous. Simply stunning. Almost all Victoria Secret model types, whereas I can't hold a candle to them.

My eyes begin to drift down to my chest as my hands lift up to cup my breasts, and I give them a little squeeze. I'm not overly large in the boobs department, but I'm considered over a handful, and they are perky. I've never felt inadequate there. My nipples are a dusky shade of pink and perk as well. Running my fingers over the sensitive nubs to make them stand up and harden, I know I don't lack in that department. They may not be huge, but they aren't small, either.

My hands begin to drift down to my flat stomach where the toned muscles flex under my own touch, causing the dangling piercing there to move hypnotically. The little gold double chain with red tear-drop diamonds drips from my navel. Jayden doesn't know about the piercing yet. He's going to have a fit and probably ask my mom to make me take it out. Sometimes, he forgets that I'm an adult. He still sees me as his kid sister.

I continue to evaluate my body, I'm of Italian descent and naturally dark, so even though the tan lines I got over the summer from laying out at our pool in the backyard are fading slightly, they are still significant. Twisting to the side, I look at my butt. Some people might call it a bubble butt, but it's from years of cheerleading in high school and having to work out constantly.

As I look over my shoulder, my hands travel around my hips to grip each hard cheek. This is the one asset I know guys like. My ass is the one thing guys comment on whenever I'm wearing my shorts or a bikini. Even the girls on my cheer squad would call me 'Cheer Butt'.

My eyes slowly close as my hands roam my body, and I try to imagine that it's Thomas's hands that caress me so softly. The sound of the water in the shower allows my mind to disappear to that place I love to escape to. The place where I'm taken whenever I read one of my romance novels.

One hand moves back around and grips my breast, sinking my digits harshly into the skin and then pinching the nipple hard. My head falls back again on my shoulders, wanting to moan loudly while I imagine it is Kyler's hand grabbing me roughly. The imagined conflicting touches elevate my growing need to come. I'm trying so hard to imagine it's their large, rough and calloused hands on me, not my petite soft ones. This isn't the first time I've masturbated to thoughts of each of them touching me. Even though usually it's one at a time, never all of them at once. This is intensifying the throbbing between my legs.

My thighs tighten automatically, trying to stave off the

growing need between them in my core. The hand on my ass slowly moves around and cups my pussy, as my breathing increases. Continuing to pinch my nipple, my vivid imagination goes crazy. In my mind's eyes, I see Jayden right in front of me, grabbing me and pushing me up against the wall with his hand around my throat, cupping my pussy and claiming it as his own. Sliding my middle finger through my slit, I begin rubbing my clit slowly.

I roll my head to the side, in efforts to aid my imagination that Jayden is nuzzling my neck. Biting and nipping at the skin there. I want to feel him suck the sensitive part below my ear into his mouth, and let him leave his marks on me. I would wear them proudly, even if I would be shunned for allowing my stepbrother, the one I basically grew up with, to claim me for everyone to see.

All I hear now in the steamy room, besides the running shower, is my heavy breathing and my heart beating rapidly in my ears. My fingers begin to rub furiously over my clit as my orgasm builds in my lower belly. Pinching my other nipple now, I shift my legs wider to give myself even more access. "Jay," I moan out in a whisper, knowing he can't hear me. "Please, Thomas."

Gripping my breast harshly, as I add another finger to rub the pulsing clit. I can feel my legs lock up as the need to come rockets through me. "Yes, Ky... more," I whisper into the empty room in a panting breath. And then I'm thrown over the side of the proverbial cliff into such an intense orgasm my hand stops and I know my fingers may leave slight bruises on my breasts.

My heavy breaths are all that's heard in the bathroom now, especially with the ringing in my ears from the blood rushing in them. Opening my eyes slowly, I look into the mirror I'm still standing in front of. My cheeks and entire body are flushed, and I'm sweating profusely now. Still breathing heavily, I drop my hands and shake my head. I watch for a little longer, seeing and feeling the droplets of sweat and moisture run down the length of my body.

Dreams and fantasies are all I will ever have of them. I really need to get Jayden past this aversion to me dating so I can at least lose my V-Card soon. Because of his overprotectiveness, I'm still a 19-year-old virgin. But not from lack of trying; it just hasn't helped that Jayden terrifies everyone who even considers trying to date me.

Shaking my head again, I turn and walk to the shower. I open the glass door and step inside, letting the water cascade down my body. Grabbing the loofa hanging from a hook on the wall, I pour a generous amount of my Jasmine body wash and begin to clean myself from all the sweat and grime, not just from my escape but also from the long day at school and the trip.

I should be thankful that despite everything, I still have Thomas as a friend, even though I would love more. I know Jayden would never allow it, and Thomas doesn't see me like that. Kyler is just Kyler... an asshole prick that doesn't even spare me a glance or time of day. And Jayden sometimes does seem like he gives a shit. I just hope they mean what they say about this trip and don't leave me out of things.

8

JAYDEN

Leaving Thomas' room with a clear plan of how this will play out, we head to the kitchen to grab something to eat. I'm unsure if Skylan is already out of the shower or still holed up in her room. Nearing the kitchen downstairs, I hear her rummaging around in the open space, which makes me smile. Just having her here brings me comfort.

Skylan enjoys cooking and baking, so I wonder what she has in store for us tonight, being our first night here. I know she's got to be tired because even as tired as I am, I'm also wired from all the planning, knowing exactly what we have in store for the next two weeks and how long it's been coming. Especially now, knowing we can take our time with this and not have to rush it.

I'm the first to round the railing, going into the kitchen with the guys close on my tail. As soon as I walk through the doorway, I stop dead in my tracks from what I see. My eyes zero in on Skylan bent over, leaning into the refrigerator with her bubble ass on full display in a pair of fucking spandex shorts. Her long, toned, and tanned legs are on full display with the slight little dip that leads from her legs to that fantastic ass of hers. I feel my cock stir in my pants, making my hand move to adjust myself immediately as my mouth goes dry at the vision of perfection bent over right in front of me. I squeeze my dick to give me a little relief, making me want to groan out loud.

I hear Thomas and Kyler come up behind me, and I feel a jolt when Thomas runs into me, making Kyler grumble under his breath about the abrupt stop. They glance over my shoulder to see what it is that I'm looking at. "Fuuuuck," Thomas hisses quietly, letting me know he's looking at the same thing I am.

Clearing my throat, I elbow him in the stomach at his obviousness. As she looks over her shoulder at us, I look away and continue moving into the kitchen. "Watch where you're going, dickhead," I grunt out, trying not to be as apparent as him that we were watching her.

"Ummm..." he coughs out. "... sorry. I guess I wasn't watching where I was... uh... going, I guess," he stammers, trying to look anywhere but at Skylan but doing everything to look guilty as hell. Her eyes are flitting back and forth between the three of us before returning to her task at hand.

Shaking her head with a smile, she sits the items on the counter that she retrieved from the refrigerator. Glancing back at Kyler, I see he has a fierce glare on his face as he walks past Thomas, slapping him on the back of the head. "Ouch, asshole," Thomas mumbles under his breath, rubbing the area that was just assaulted as we all sit at the island counter.

"What 'cha making there, sweetness?" I question, looking over the items she has sat out. She bends over again, pulling out a wooden cutting board, and then extracts a butcher knife from the drawer. Pulling a green pepper from the pile of items and slicing it up on the cutting board, she smiles at me.

"I'm thinking fajitas. It's quick and easy, plus it's filling and can feed all of us," she says, cutting the green peppers into slices along with the red peppers and onions. Just from her cutting up the vegetables, the smell permeates the air.

"Hell yeah," Thomas reacts, slapping the counter as he sits in one of the stools, making Kyler glance at him. Skylan glances over at Thomas with a little laugh at his enthusiasm. "You know I love your cooking, Butterfly."

Ignoring Thomas's outburst, I focus back on the brunette beauty, who is still smiling at the praise and attention she's getting. It just reminds me how awful I usually am around her whenever I have friends over.

"That sounds great for our first night," I smile. "By the way my dad just called," I inform her. I'm hoping she takes this news well. Being stuck here with me and my friends probably wasn't top of her list of things, but we're going to make sure this is the best holiday she's ever had, and this is just the beginning.

After slicing up the vegetables and meat, she turns to grab the pan to fry everything. The stove knob clicks as she turns it on, and I watch as she pours a little olive oil into the pan. Stretching on her tippy toes, she tucks the oil back in the cabinet above her head. Turning back around, she turns that full watt smile on me, sending my heart into palpitations. I love it when that smile is turned toward me, which lately it rarely is, so when it is, I love to see it and try to commit it to memory. "Really? What did he say?" she asks, as she leans her elbows on the counter, giving me her full attention.

Tilting my head to the side, trying to look disappointed and upset, I answer her. "Unfortunately, they can't get a flight out of Chicago because of the weather," I say, and her face falls slightly. "So they aren't going to make it. It's just going to be us."

"But it's Christmas, Jay," she says, sounding sad. This will be the first Christmas of us not being all together, so I know she's upset.

"I know, Sky. But we will all make sure this is a great holiday. Just the four of us," I say, looking at the guys. "Right, guys?"

She looks over to Thomas, who gives her a huge, goofy smile and nods. "Absolutely. It will be a blast just us four," Thomas says excitedly. A small smile begins to creep up the sides of her mouth. When her eyes flit to Kyler, he just gives her a subtle nod, and instantly, the growing smile is gone.

Her eyes slowly make their way to me, and I smirk at her, giving her a little wink. Her face brightens. "Okay. As long as you guys don't ignore me like usual and just do guy stuff," she says, looking between the three of us but then focusing on me.

"Of course, not sweetness. We will make sure this is a holiday none of us will forget," I say, and she nods, happy with that response. As she turns back to toss the peppers, onions, and meat combination into the pan along with her seasonings, I look over to Thomas and Kyler. Thomas still has a playful smile, but Kyler's eyes darken, and his devious half-smirk forms as he looks at me.

Tonight changes everything for all of us.

Skylan

Sitting the last plate in front of Thomas, I sit down next to him with my own and we dig in. It's almost like they haven't eaten in days the way they devour the food. I fork a few vegetables and the meat into the soft tortilla and lift it to my lips taking a small bite letting the flavor erupt on my tongue. I'm not a big eater as it is, and it's getting late, so I don't want to eat too much because it will cause me an upset stomach and keep me awake.

"Damn, Butterfly. This is delicious," Thomas says, smiling over at me. "I mean I've had your cooking before but this right here is restaurant quality."

I can feel my cheeks heat with the praise and smile at him. His blonde hair flopping into his milk chocolate eyes. "Thanks, Bear," I say, using the nickname that I hold for when it's just us. I see Jayden and Kyler's head quickly move in our direction, but I don't pay them any attention.

"I mean it. You really have a talent with cooking," he says as he bumps my shoulder with his. I immediately look back down to my plate and lift the little tortilla fajita back to my lips smiling.

Kyler's head slowly moves back to focus on his food with a deep scowl on his face. I'm sure he just doesn't want me in their vicinity, but too damn bad. This is my house too and he needs to get used to it.

Jayden's eyes are still flitting between Thomas and I. I can see the question in them. Thomas is either ignoring the look or doesn't even register it. "Bear?" he says in a gruff voice. "What the fuck does that mean?" Jayden asks, making both of us look over at him.

Thomas chuckles as he grabs a napkin to wipe his mouth before answering. The hardness in Jayden's eyes make me not want to answer but for some damn reason Thomas thinks it's funny.

Jayden's eyes bore into mine as Thomas answers. "It's because of the bear hugs I give her in class. And since I call her Butterfly, she joked one time calling me bear, and it just stuck, I guess," he explains.

"Fucking bullshit," I barely hear the words leaving Kyler's lips before he stuffs more food into his mouth. Jayden's eyes flit to Kyler and my brother shakes his head. Focusing back on my food, I ignore them for the rest of dinner.

After I finish the little that I put on my plate, I stand grabbing my glass and taking it over to the sink. Immediately coming up behind me is Jayden, sitting his dishes in as well. He kisses the top of my head softly. "Thanks, Sweetness. Dinner was delicious," he whispers in my hair.

"You're welcome. You know I love to cook," I reply quietly.

"I appreciate you doing it."

Looking over my shoulder at the other two as they are just finishing up as well. "Just leave the dishes. I can clean up," I say to them, and they both nod standing from the island counter.

"Are you going to be okay here by yourself for a little while? With the storm coming, I'm worried we won't have enough provisions to keep us for two whole weeks. The guys and I are heading back to the store really quick to grab a few more things," Jayden says as he leans his back against the counter I'm standing at.

Glancing back over my shoulder, I see Kyler and Thomas standing near the entrance of the kitchen area eyeing each other. Thomas has his head down with a small smirk on his lips and Kyler is glaring at him. I wonder what that's about.

Finally focusing back on my stepbrother standing so close to me, I look up into his molten brown eyes that look like warm milk chocolate. I nod slightly as I turn around to grab the other dishes on the counter. "Yeah. I'll be fine. I'm just going to clean up here and then go call Kenzi before bed," I say.

He studies me for a moment, then leans down and kisses the top of my head again. "Okay. Stay inside, please. We won't be too long," he says, pushing off the counter toward the guys.

"Mhmm," I mumble. Glancing over my shoulder as they leave, I see Kyler push Thomas ahead of him, mumbling, "Fucking bear. You wish." I hear Thomas cackle at the interaction as he jogs to the entrance. My brow furrows at the way he's acting. Jayden looks back just before walking through the doorway and gives me a little smile, which I return.

Turning back to the sink, I grip the sides of the counter again and shake my head slowly. I'm so fucking confused with all of this. Why is Kyler acting like more of a dick than usual? My spirits drop slightly, wondering if what I thought would be an epic holiday with my family is going to be such a letdown. I'm just in their way of fun and bringing them down.

9

SKYLAN

Once the dishes are done and put away, I wipe down the counters, making sure everything is as it was when we got here. I hate waking up to a dirty kitchen. Looking around the kitchen area, I dry my hands off on the light blue kitchen towel then drape it over the sink. As I walk by the kitchen island I push in the chairs that we all sat on.

Walking through the kitchen entrance, I switch off the lights and head toward the front door. Glancing outside, I look where Jayden's car was parked, seeing they are still gone. It didn't take me long to clean up, so I knew they wouldn't be back yet. I don't know why I looked, just making sure I guess. I'm not scared of staying here by myself, I just feel like they probably could have taken me with them if they really wanted to.

Rounding the banister, I slowly head up the stairs to my room. Switching the hallway light off, I turn into my room and close the door. The house is so quiet with just me roaming around. Walking to my bed, I throw myself across it sideways, bouncing on the dark pink comforter as I reach for my phone on the side dresser.

Clicking the side button on my phone, the screen illuminates and I see several missed calls and messages from my best friend, Kenzi and Bri, plus other social media messages and notifications. I figured I would deal with Kenzi first so I open her messages first. As I go through them, I laugh at each one.

> Kenzi: How did the drive go?

> Kenzi: Take a trip with 3 hot guys and you're ignoring me now?

> Kenzi: ???

> Kenzi: Are you okay? I'm worried.

The last one came in a few minutes before I got to my room. I chuckle at how she gets so quickly. I roll over onto my back, lifting my knees with my feet planted on the bed. Lifting the phone above my face, I smile as I reply to her.

> Me: I'm okay. Sorry, after unpacking we made dinner. Are you all packed and ready to fly out tomorrow?

Just a few seconds after I hit send, the three little dots begin to bounce indicating Kenzi is replying.

> Kenzi: Yep. All ready. How's it going over there?

Starting to type out my reply, then I delete it. I wonder if all that has happened can be told in a text message. Typing it out again, then deleting. Biting my bottom lip, I type my final quick message to my best friend.

Me: Can I call u?

Still biting my bottom lip, I stare at my phone waiting for her to respond. My phone rings instead. Turning over onto my stomach, kicking my feet up I swipe the green button answering the call. "Hey, Kenz," I say as I answer.

"Bitch. How's everything going up there?" I hear her moving around her room. I'm sure she's still packing. Releasing a deep breath, I shake my head.

"Honestly, I don't know how I'm going to do this for two whole weeks. And I know you hate hearing about it, too... but fucking Kyler and Thomas together with Jayden. What the actual fuck?" I say, dropping my head on top of my comforter. Groaning out loud, I throw myself once again on my back, but throw my arm over my forehead.

I know it bothers her to hear about the crushes I have on Thomas and Kyler, especially with Jayden around them because she has her own little obsession with him. Hell, I have a little crush on my step brother as well, but I won't tell her that. Kenzi would be upset. Along with the fact how weird it is since we basically grew up together. It also sounds pathetic to my own ears, knowing how much they are all out of my league.

"You know how protective Jay gets. He says he will make sure we all have fun together while we're here, and he won't leave me out. But Thomas was talking to me at dinner and I swear Jay wanted to kill him," I explain. "Kyler didn't say much at all the entire trip, but hot damn," I say, fanning my face, "What I would give just to get those steel blue eyes on me," I give a little moan as I think about him.

"Bitch... when you choose to crush on a guy, you aim high. I swear all the girls at school are after Kyler. And Thomas isn't lacking in that department either," she replies.

"Look who's talking," I say laughing. "But seriously. I have a feeling this trip is going to be so boring. They are going to spend the entire time playing video games or pool or something else that has nothing to do with me."

"I don't think Jayden would isolate you while you guys are there. And you and Thomas are friends, I don't see him doing that to you," she says, trying to settle my worries and alleviate any anxiety I'm having. It somewhat helps, but after they left for the store by themselves without inviting me, I'm starting to second guess his promise.

"Yeah I know. But being cooped up here with all three of them together is going to be torture. Especially when I want to jump two of them," I say with a light-hearted chuckle. And actually I wouldn't mind either of the three, but again I can't say that to her, or anyone.

A creak from just outside my door catches my ear as the words leave my lips. I shoot straight up in bed, looking in that direction. My eyes are wide and I'm trying to concentrate on the sounds around me. The silence in the house is so loud in my ears. Now I'm wishing I left the hallway light on so I can see anything moving about outside my door.

"Oh trus–" Kenzi starts, but I cut her off.

"Shhh!"

Quietly I stand from my bed and walk slowly and as silently as possible to the door. Goosebumps rise all over my body and my heartrate kicks up a notch. I'm not sure if it's fear or just adrenaline. Pressing my ear against the wood, I try to listen for any more movement. When no other sounds are heard, I gently take the door knob in my sweaty palm and wrench the door open fiercely to find no one standing outside it. Poking my head out of the door, I look both ways into the hallway and see nothing, so I close the door and return to my bed, shaking my head. Had to be either in my head or the house was just settling.

"What is it?" Kenzi whispers into the phone.

"I don't know. I thought I heard someone outside of my bedroom, but the guys left to the store a bit ago," I say shrugging, as if she can see me. I focus back on my phone and the conversation with Kenzi. "Anyways, I'm sure it will all be okay. I'm just frustrated being around them, you know?"

"I get it. I'm sure it will go much better than you're expecting," she says as I nod and yawn. We talk for a little while longer while she finishes getting packed up for her trip home. I promise to call her in a couple of days. I want to make sure she gets settled in at her parents' house.

After we hang up, I lay across my bed once again. Stretching to grab the cord to my charger, I plug my phone in. It's already low on battery due to being at school all day and then the trip.

Slowly I sit back up and listen quietly once again to the silence in the house. I'm sure I heard something before, like someone walking outside my door. But now, the cabin is eerily quiet. I have to take into consideration that this is a cabin, and the wood makes noises all the time.

I decide to go investigate a little further. Maybe the guys are playing a trick on me or something. Trying to scare me. Slowly I stand and walk to the door, opening it without any noise. Stepping out of my room, I pad across the hall to Jayden's door. Leaning close, I press my ear to see if I hear any voices or noises within. Totally quiet. I knock softly on his door. "Jayden, are you in there?" I call out with no response.

The door to our adjoining bathroom in my room was open, so I know he wasn't in there taking a shower. I ease his door open and glance around. Not finding him in there, I close the door softly with a barely audible click and walk to the other side of the upstairs where Thomas and Kyler's rooms are. All the lights are out, and I begin shivering at the coldness settling in.

I pass Kyler's room, and only slow down to listen if I hear any voices, but when I hear nothing I continue to Thomas' door. "Thomas..." I call out and knock softly. "...can I come in?" I ask, standing there listening quietly. I press my ear to the door and concentrate on any noises I hear. I knock once again, and nothing.

Standing up straight, I look back down the dark hall. Wishing I had changed into sweats or at the very least some pajama pants, these spandex shorts aren't enough. Goosebumps rise all over my body as I shiver again. Wrapping my arms around myself, I head back to the stairs and listen to the quiet in the house. Hoping to hear one of their voices, but all I hear is the howling of the wind outside.

Standing at the top of the stairs, I feel the chill run through me again. This time not just from the cold sliding through the house but also from how alone I feel in this large house in a secluded part of the mountains. Gingerly I walk down the stairs, and glance over the side of the stairs into the main living area, but it's dark and I can't see anything.

Moving to the front door, I look out the main windows again. Jayden's Acura still isn't there. I wonder how long they will be gone. Checking the lock on the front door once again, even though I know I locked it previously. Grabbing the sweatshirt that was hanging by the door, I slip it over my head. By the smell of it, it must be Jayden's.

Lifting the collar of the shirt up to my nose, I inhale deeply at the scent of his cologne, Black Phantom. The scent invades my nostrils and immerses me in his smell. Releasing a sigh, I move back up the stairs to my room.

Walking around to the opposite side of the bed, I sit and pick up my phone. Dialing Jayden's number, I lift the phone to my ear and listen to it ring. It rings only once and it goes to voicemail. Maybe he left it here or maybe it died. I hang up and look through my contacts again and press Thomas' number. This time, it rings and rings... and then goes to voicemail. After hanging up, I try again immediately. This time, it goes directly to voicemail.

"What the fuck is going on?" I say, staring at my phone. Taking into consideration that we're in a secluded area of Gatlinburg, there's a chance they may not have reception. Looking through my contacts once again, my finger hovers over Kyler's name. He doesn't know that I have his number. I had taken it from Jayden's phone a while ago just in case. They are best friends. The excuse I gave for keeping the number is that I might need to contact him in case of an emergency. I hesitate even longer before finally giving in and pressing the green button.

Lifting the phone to my ear, my knee jumps up and down. My nerves are shot and I don't know whether I want him to answer or not. But that thought is short lived, when the call is immediately sent to voicemail again. As soon as I disconnect, my hand drops to my lap and I stare down at the phone.

When I lift the phone to try Jayden's number again, the lights in my room go out. I gasp and jumped to my feet holding my phone close to my chest. Without any lights from anywhere, the room is thrown into complete darkness.

Standing next to my bed, the only light is from the moon coming in my window. Slowly walking to the door, I try to listen. Unsure what to listen for if the guys aren't here. In this situation, I would typically use the flashlight on my phone right now, but I'm too terrified to even try.

Hearing the sound of the wind coming through the front door as someone opens it, I stop immediately. Again... I listen. I hear it softly click shut, and I release a breath in a huff. It must be the guys.

"Jayden," I yell out and then wait. Nothing. "Jayden... is that you?" I call out again even louder, but I can hear the shakiness in my voice. But still nothing.

Slowly I walk over to the door again. Opening the door and stepping into the hall, I begin moving down the hall staying close against the wall as I head toward the stairs. I peek around the corner where the front door is still closed. Unable to see anything else, except the moonlight shining in through the windows of the front. Moving around the corner, I lean against the wall and close my eyes. I take in a deep, quiet breath then slowly release it.

Now I'm wondering if the sounds I heard were just my imagination. Taking in another deep breath, I move to walk down the stairs. Moving slowly and as quietly as I can, I don't move my eyes from the closed door. Stepping on the landing, I check the door and it's not locked. *What. The. Fuck.* I click the lock in place once again.

A scraping sound comes from behind me, and I spin around, looking toward the kitchen. The ability to breath leaves me as I'm held in fear. The moon slightly illuminates the large bay windows from the kitchen and I can see the silhouette of someone standing in the kitchen doorway not moving.

"Jay?" I whisper, not loud enough for them to hear. "Is that you?"

The figure in the doorway wears a dark hoodie with the

hood covering their head. Just standing there. I can't see their face because it's too damn dark.

I slowly take a step back, still grasping my phone against my chest. With my other hand, I reach behind me as I take another step trying to feel for the banister.

"T-Thomas... Th-This isn't funny," I say, stuttering over my words as I step up on the first stair. The figure casually tilts its head to the side, still looking at me but not moving. I take another step up the stairs. My heart is racing and feels like it's trying to beat right out of my chest. Shudders run through my entire body.

Hoping it's just the guys playing a trick on me, I take in a deep breath and release it trying to calm myself. I don't know how it could be anyone other than them, but wonder why they would be doing this? As I feel the fear racing through my body, the fact that my pussy is tingling is so confusing. I've read about this type of thing in some of my books, and the thought always turned me on. But having it actually happen to me is terrifying, and yet my fucking body isn't getting the memo that this is real not a goddamn book.

"Who... Who are you?" I ask, and they straighten their head but still don't move. As I move up the steps, their head follows my movement. Taking another step, lights on their mask illuminate making me jump and halt where I stand halfway up the stairs. There are two white x's where the eyes are and a creepy cross-stitch looking smile stretching across the bottom for the mouth. "This isn't funny," I yell, and they slowly move their head back and forth as if to say no. The dominating aura and control this guy has is stifling.

The dark figure finally takes a step forward as I near the top of the stairs, making me stop. I know I should move quickly, but fear has me rooted in place. Shaking my head trying to dispel my thoughts, because I'm wondering why this fear has my body so wired, and turned on. As I'm stuck where I'm at, he continues to move reaching the bottom of the stairs. Grabbing the banister with both hands, he slowly begins to step up them, as his hands glide along the wooden rail. Even in the darkness, the lights from his mask shine on the stairs and his hands. It's then that I notice, he's also wearing black gloves and his hands look enormous.

"Wh-what do you want?" I whisper. Clutching the phone to my chest, I glance over toward mine and Jayden's rooms. I can make if I could just fucking move and lock myself in.

As he slowly moves up the stairs, he still hasn't uttered one word. "My brother and his friends will be here any minute. If you leave now I won't tell anyone," I say, finally hearing a low chuckle from the dark bulky figure. The sound is so deep it reverberates through my body. "What do you want?" I yell, stepping up to the top landing.

He is only four or five steps from me, still moving slowly like he doesn't have a care in the world. Like I didn't just threaten him with my brother, Kyler and Thomas. A deep rumble of a voice comes through, but I can tell that it's altered or changed somehow, when he finally answers with just one word.

"You."

With that one word, I take off down the hall to my room. I slam the door closed and turn quickly to lock it. The locks on these damn doors are so insignificant. They were made to keep nosey brothers and sisters out, not intruders.

Slowly I back away with my eyes glued to the wooden barrier between the masked man and myself. The house is still silent, and my room is pitch black and dark. Glancing around the room, I look for some kind of weapon, but there isn't anything. Looking to my left, I see my bathroom door is still open. "Shit," I whisper as I move quickly to close it, but I'm too late.

Just before I get to the door he's walking through it, hitting the door making it bang against the wall. A little shriek leaves my lips as I stumble backwards toward my bed.

"Please don't," I whisper out in a breath. The back of my eyes sting with tears. I don't even know what I'm asking for or what I'm begging for him not to do.

My eyes jump over to the door and I move into action before my brain even catches up. I'm in flight mode, since I know due to his size, I definitely can't fight him. Running toward the door, but before I even get close I feel a sharp sting at the back of my head as I'm jerked backward from him grabbing my hair.

My hands immediately fly to where he's holding my hair at the back of my head, making me drop my phone. I hear it clatter to the floor as his free hand wraps around my waist, lifting me up from the ground. I start kicking and screaming as he turns around and heads back to my bed. As terrified as I am, I'm also turned on which feels like such a contradiction. My inner turmoil is confusing the fuck out of me and making everything worse.

Kicking back trying to get any traction against him as I can, but since I don't have any shoes on it really isn't doing much to this gigantic beast of a man. He's huge with a broad chest and muscular arms. Even with him holding me against his chest, he still towers over me. He throws me on my bed, and I try to scramble away from him as soon as I hit it, but he grabs me by my ankles and pulls me back to him.

"Uh, uh, uh," he mutters darkly with a little chuckle. He's barely breathing heavy and now this close I can tell his voice is somewhat distorted, sounding almost electronic.

He kneels one knee on my bed between my legs and

grabs my hair at the base of my skull, pinning me down to the mattress. My hands move to grab onto the comforter, but he's too strong and he holds me in place.

"Please... no... please don't..." I stumble my words out trying anything right now. I still don't know what I'm asking him not to do, and these conflicting feelings inside me aren't helping matters what so fucking ever. "You can't... you just... please don't... p-please," I hoarsely beg against the bed.

Lifting his other leg up he spreads my legs wide and grinds down on top of my ass. Fucking hell, he's hard and huge there too. This is a beast of a man in every way.

"Fuck," he growls out as he moves closer to my ear. "I love to hear you beg, little whore." His voice sounds deep even through the distortion. "Now it just depends..." he takes a deep breath through his nose, almost sounding as if he's... smelling me. "...whether you give me what I want or I just take it. But that's up to you."

The hand in my hair tightens, and I try to shake my head, but with him tightening his hold again, I can't move. All I can think about is I'm about to lose my virginity to this asshole. How is this fair? I've been saving that for someone who I deemed special. Someone I care about. I knew it was a little stupid and probably very naive, but it should still be my choice regardless.

"No, please...," I beg, my voice low and shaky. Tears begin to stream from my eyes, wetting my comforter. Where the hell is Jayden and the guys? Why aren't they back yet?

"I know you want this..." he says chuckling. "...you like the chase to get that tight little pussy of yours wet, don't you?" he asks, and I stop moving, stunned silent. My eyes widen and I freeze. At my reaction he laughs darkly. Moving his legs, he spreads my legs even further apart. And right about now I'm wishing I had changed into those sweatpants. "Now... let's see how right I am."

My head shakes feverishly trying to not only deter him from doing what I think he's going to but also hopefully will the wetness that is most definitely in my panties away. I feel him move behind me, but he has such a hold on my head, I can feel strands of my hair pull out.

Moving my t-shirt up a bit, he slides his bare hand over my waist. I suck in a breath at his touch. He must have removed his glove. Sliding his hand under me and into the front of my shorts, he dips them under my lace panties. Squeezing my eyes shut and biting down on my bottom lip trying not to cry, I feel him move his fingers through my folds and he groans loudly.

Embarrassment floods my system. I feel like such a freak. I try to close my legs, but he's too strong and his thighs are massive holding my legs apart. As he forces his fingers roughly over my clit and shoving two of his fingers through my wetness, I hear him release a hiss as I whimper.

I taste copper as I bite my lip trying not to moan at the feeling running through my core. I can feel myself getting even wetter as he continues to rub over that little bundle of nerves that has never been touched by anyone but myself.

He groans loudly. "Fuck... you are soaking wet for me, little whore," he says, and I try to shake my head. He laughs. "You can't deny this," he says, pulling his fingers from inside my shorts. He wipes my obvious arousal over my lips. Squeezing my eyes shut once again for what feels like the hundredth time, I try to move my head away but he has such a tight hold I am unable to budge. All I can do is squirm under him, but he just continues to grind his hard cock on my ass.

He moans as I hear him making sure I know he's sucking

his fingers clean of my wetness. "Mmmmm. You taste like the darkest shade of sin with the sweetest flavor innocence all wrapped up in one. And I can't wait to wreck you."

As soon as the words leave his lips, lights shine through my window. A sob leaves my throat and tears start to fall heavily. The guys are back. I know that's them coming down the gravel drive and I feel the sweetest bit of relief course through my veins. The masked intruder leans down, pressing me into the bed with his massive weight even more than before, and pushes his mask right next to my ear. I can hear him breathing heavily, even with the voice distorter.

"If you even think about telling anyone about me, little whore, I will make you regret it. And you won't even see me coming... Neither will they. Trust me," he growls into my ear, making me tremble . "Got me?"

All I can do is squeeze my eyes shut and try to nod as best as I can with him still holding my hair so tightly. He grips harshly pulling my head back at an awkward angle. I want to scream from the searing pain in my scalp but all I do is whimper.

"Fucking say it," he demands in a much harsher tone. Shaking all over with the mixture of fear and arousal, I'm trembling so hard I can feel it all the way down to my bones.

"I... I won't say anything. P-promise." He pushes my head down into the mattress roughly before letting my hair go.

The weight from my back disappears, and I hear footsteps quickly move away, and out of my room. I can tell by the heaviness of the steps, he's running down the stairs. Quiet sobs wrack my body and I break as the tears continue to flow. Rolling onto my side, I curl into a ball and silently cry.

10

THOMAS

" **A** re you absolutely sure about this, Jay?" I ask Jayden quietly staring straight ahead as he pulls into the little open garage and parks his Acura. Almost as if I speak any louder it will make this situation even more real. As he puts the car in park and pushes the button to shut it off, I look over at him to survey his reactions. Laying his head back on the headrest and closing his eyes, I hear him release a long breath. I can tell this maybe how he feels this needs to be done like Kyler does, but I know it's bothering him just as much as it does me.

I'm down for whatever they need, but I just want to make sure she will be okay with this in the long run and it will be safe. I meant what I told him before. I care about Skylan. The only thing that held me back from asking her out and pursuing something with the beautiful woman she's become, was the fact that she's Jayden's little sister and I didn't want to jeopardize our friendship or their relationship.

"It will work. This was only step one. Now, we need to see how things pan out," he says. Staring at him from my seat, the silence surrounds us like a heavy blanket. "It has to," he says on a quiet breath, almost to himself. He takes another deep breath, and without looking over at me he reaches for the door handle and steps out of the SUV. Shaking my head as his door closes, I reluctantly get out.

Jayden and I grab the few bags of stuff we got from the little convenient store down the street and approach the front door. We had to come back with something, or the reason we left would have been questioned. Jayden inserts the key and turns the knob. I hear quiet footsteps approach from the side of the house as Kyler walks up beside us, sliding on a blue and gold Georgia Tech hoodie. Jayden and I turn our heads toward him, and he gives a little nod with a stoic look on his face. Jayden hands him a couple of the bags as we step inside. Closing the door behind us, I look up the stairs noticing lights are on in the hallway between all the rooms.

I hand the bags in my hands off to Jayden. "I'm going to go check on her, " I say, making my way to the stairs leading to our rooms. As soon as I take two steps up, I hear Jayden speak.

"Remember how this goes, T. Don't say shit," he growls out. I furrow my brow and glare at him. Kyler steps in front of Jayden toward the stairs, glaring up at me.

"Don't fuck this up for me, Thomas. I swear to—"

"I fucking told you I got it, Ky," I interrupt him. I take the few steps back down to advance on him. "And this isn't just about *just* you anymore. It's about all of us now," I correct him, standing toe to toe as he glares right back at me. We are close in height, but he is slightly taller, but has a hell of a lot more mass than me. I'm lean and fit where he's bulky and muscular. I've wanted Skylan for as long as I can remember, so I'm not going to do anything to jeopardize this but I also won't allow them to hurt her either.

Jayden steps up next to us. Kyler and I are in a stare down, and neither of us loses our focus. "Cool it, guys. We're in this together, remember," he says quietly, trying to calm the situation.

Finally releasing the stare down, I can still see the tension physically rolling off of Kyler. The edginess in his demeanor is tangible. Jayden can see it as well, so he shifts the bags he's holding into one hand and claps me on the shoulder.

"Go," he orders, inclining his head motioning toward the stairs. "Go check on her. Meet back in Kyler's room in thirty minutes to let us know how she is," Jayden tells me, but I don't respond. I'm too wound up. As I turn to go up the stairs, I see Jayden grasp the back of Kyler's neck and guide him to the kitchen. I'm sure he's going to try and calm him down. If anyone is going to fuck this up, it will be Kyler with his temper and anger issues.

Stepping up to Skylan's slightly open door, I can see the small table lamp light on. I knock lightly. "Sky... we're back," I say softly as I push the door further open. When I step in through the little opening, my heart sinks as her head pops up from under the blanket. Her face is blotchy, eyes are red rimmed and watery so I can tell she's been crying. She sits up as I walk closer to the bed. Sitting down on the edge, I lean in closer to her. She wipes her face trying to hide the still falling tears and crosses her legs in front of her under the comforter.

"What's wrong, Butterfly? Why are you crying?" I ask, trying to act oblivious to the situation. Lifting my hand, I wipe more tears from her face. I let the back of my hand linger on the swell of her cheeks more than necessary, just wanting to feel her soft skin. I know what the fuck is wrong, at least I can guess what Kyler did to her, but now I have to act like I have no idea. My heart beats a thousand miles an hour in my chest, feeling like it wants to jump right out and connect with hers.

Looking up at me, her mouth opens and closes like she wants to tell me something, but hesitates. I can see the turmoil in her eyes. I know he threatened her to not tell anyone, but it still bothers me that she feels she can't confide in me. I'm not sure if she did actually tell me, would I tell the guys or not. Finally releasing a heavy breath, she gives me a small smile shaking her head.

"It's stupid," she says, giving a little chuckle looking down at her lap. Cupping her chin gently, I lift her gaze to meet mine. Her dark brown eyes search my face as I know mine are doing the same.

"It can't be stupid if it has you this upset. What happened? You can talk to me," I say. She takes in a deep breath and releases it in a burst. Now I have the inner warring of sides, wanting her to tell me to satisfy the need of her to trust me and the side for her not to, in order to prove this is something she does want like the guys say and it's not all in vain.

"I was talking to Kenzi, and after I got off the phone with her I thought I heard some noises downstairs. And with you guys gone," she shrugs her shoulders. "I guess I just got a little freaked out by myself here," she finishes.

I sit there staring at her a little longer. Cupping her cheeks with both hands, I stare into her big doe eyes. Eyes I could get lost in for hours. I use my thumbs to wipe the rest of the tears from under her eyes and on her cheeks. "You sure that's all?" I ask her, still trying to see if she will tell me... if she would trust me. I'm not sure even if she did, if I would tell Jay and Kyler that she said anything.

She sniffs a little, and gives me another small smile. "Yep. That's all. See? Stupid, right?" she says with a tinkling little laugh. Smiling at her, I pull her face to mine, kissing her sweetly on her forehead. I take a deep breath, smelling the scent of her Jasmine and Vanilla scented shampoo.

"Not stupid. Being secluded up here can be a bit intimidating. Next time we will take you with us, okay?" I say and she nods at me. Standing from her bed, I look down at where she's sitting and give her a small smile.

She looks up at me with an innocent smile on her beautiful face. "Now, get some sleep. We were talking about going for a little hike tomorrow. You are going to need your rest," I tell her, and she nods again. Laying down and settling into her bed, I pull the comforter up over her and tuck her in. Leaning down, I shut the table lamp light off, throwing the room into darkness with a little click. The only light is from the hallway pouring in from her open door.

I glance back down to her, and see she's still watching me. Knowing I need to leave before I do or say more, I turn and walk to her door.

"Thomas," I hear her call out just before I pull the door closed. I turn and look at her, trying not to look as guilty as I feel right now. I smile at her. "Thanks," she says, shyly. I give her a little wink, with a small smile raising the corners of lips.

"Anything for you, Butterfly. Now sleep," I say, closing the door quietly behind me.

I walk with a heavy heart down to Kyler's room to see if they made it up here yet. It hasn't been thirty minutes, so they could still be downstairs. I open his door and look around, but the room is completely empty.

Closing the door, I make my way back downstairs. Kyler and Jayden are standing at the island counter, both with glasses of what appears to be whiskey in their hands. Walking over, I grab a glass from inside the cabinet and pour myself three fingers of the expensive whiskey they have open on the counter. I take a long drink before looking at them. They are already staring expectantly at me.

Gently placing the glass on the counter in front of me, I look over at them. "She didn't say shit to me. She was still crying though," I say looking at Jayden. Turning my head to glare over at Kyler, I ask, "What the fuck went down?"

Kyler takes a drink and then gives us a quick rundown of what happened and what he said and did to her. Shaking my head at him the entire time, because he's telling the fucking story like he's reading a goddamn newpaper. No emotion in at all.

"And that doesn't fucking bother you? That she's fucking scared now," I whisper shout. I don't want her to overhear us discussing this. I know she's still upstairs because I would have heard her door open.

Kyler leans on the counter and drops his head down. He releases a heavy breath, shaking his head slightly. "Of course, it fucking bothers me," he says looking up at me. "But I know Sky wants this too."

"You *assume*," I grit out the last word. "You fucking assume... you don't know," I say incredulously. "She hasn't come out and told you that she wants to be stalked, chased and *attacked*," I hiss out the last word. "What the actual fuck?" I say, throwing my hands up in the air. This delusional asshole. He's projecting his needs onto Skylan.

Slowly Kyler lifts his head, looking at me with a new fury in his eyes, but I don't back down. I won't. He's still leaning heavily on the counter as he bares his teeth at me.

And I'm sure if this counter wasn't between us, he would surely come at me. Jayden is just standing there next to Kyler, watching everything quietly.

"Actually, asshole, she has," he says, then hesitates. "I mean, she hasn't told me directly but..." he trails off shrugging his shoulders. I look between him and Jayden.

"But? But what dickhead? Have you two neglected to fill me in on this part?" I say, slamming my palm down on the counter. "This sounds like a crucial part of the fucking plan, don't ya think?" My voice is getting louder by the end of my rant.

"Hold it the fuck down, or she will come down here," Jayden whisper shouts at me, looking past me at the kitchen entrance, like she's about to walk in at any moment. Glaring at both of them, I stand up straight, folding my arms across my chest. We are not going any further until they give me all the information.

"Why don't you two fill me in on this missing piece of information? You expect me to be all in, but you don't want to give me all the fucking details," I say, looking between the two of them. Jayden looks to Kyler, who, in turn, looks back at him. They always seem to communicate in that crazy silent way until Jayden gives a slight shrug of his shoulders and nods at Kyler.

Once again, Kyler drops his head trying to regain his composure. Releasing a heavy breath, he finally looks up at me through his lashes. The anger he had just a moment ago seems to have dissipated, but his tight posture is still tense.

"I was in the library," he breathes out, shaking his head slightly and beginning his story. "I heard Sky's voice in the aisle next to the one I was in and looked through the books to see who she was talking to. She didn't know I was there, but she was with Bri, and she was explaining a dream she had about some book she had read. She was holding this book... The Hunting or Haunting of something or someone, I don't fucking remember," he says, getting frustrated. While he's explaining it, I lift my glass once again taking a huge drink of the amber liquid trying to calm my nerves. The burn going down no longer effects me. I don't know if it's from the amount I've drunk already or my body being so wired. "Sky was telling Bri about how this book turned her on, and she wished she had someone who would stalk her like the guy in the book did. Someone to pursue her and chase her down, to make her... *submit*," he drops his voice to a deep gruff sound on the final word.

My mouth is gaped open with all these revelations. I would have never guessed my sweet Butterfly would be into stuff like this. I'm shocked right now to hear this kind of stuff turns her on. Granted, I can understand. Hell, it kind of turns me on too, so I can see how it can be appealing for sure. And who am I to kink shame.

"So... what gave you this little idea for the two of you, well... the three of us now, to do this? Why not just ask her or talk to her to see if she would like to do it?" I ask. That would be the simple way, right? Not taking the chance of fucking her up for real if she was only into the fantasy of it. Not the reality.

Kyler releases a frustrated breath. "Because, this way, it would be more authentic. We give her what she's looking for... and I get what I need, also." My brow furrows at the last statement.

"What *you* need? What the fuck does that mean?" I ask him, as I grab my glass and the bottle of whiskey again, pouring myself another healthy serving. I'm typically not a drinker but this has my nerves on edge right now. I am not feeling anything like myself at the moment. I'm usually the one who laughs everything off. The jokester. The light-hearted playful friend. None of this was on my end of the year bingo card.

Kyler glares at me. He seems unsure about explaining this part to me. I raise one eyebrow at him while I wait for his explanation. "Either you fucking explain everything to me, or I'm done with this. So, it's your choice," I say, crossing my arms over my chest.

11

KYLER

"You can trust him, Ky," Jayden leans over, speaking to me quietly. Looking over at my best friend, I nod. Calling him my best friend doesn't exactly cover it. He's grown as close as a brother to me the last few years, and he knows everything about me. From my family issues to my sexual predilections. I know I need to tell Thomas, but I feel like a freak whenever I try to explain it. That's why I usually just... don't.

Releasing a deep sigh, I finish off the rest of the strong whiskey in my glass feeling the burn all the way to my stomach then look over the counter to Thomas. Gently I sit the glass down on the granite and grip the edges trying to stave off the apprehension I'm feeling right now. I don't talk about this part of me to anyone but Jayden.

"Fine," I say releasing a heavy breath. "I have a..." I hesitate momentarily. Knowing he is going to judge me, I still keep going because this needs to be said. "Have you ever heard of a primal kink?" I tilt my head inquisitively, as I ask Thomas. His brow furrows slightly and when he doesn't reply right away, I continue. "It's where you enjoy hunting down your partner, and taking them on more of a primal level... aggressively fucking them and having them fight you off. It's the thrill of the hunt that gets my blood pumping, but it's previously consented..." At those last few words Thomas opens his mouth ready to object with how we're going about this with Skylan. "...or at least you know it's what they want beforehand," I amend the last part in a sardonic way, making him close his mouth.

Thomas looks between Jayden and me. He scratches his head, probably trying to wrap his mind around it. Staying quiet, I give him the time he needs to understand or at the very least put together his own thoughts, so that he can ask whatever questions he may have. My hands grip the counter, turning my knuckles white, from the restlessness inside me waiting on his reply.

"So, kind of like... um... forced sex fantasy?" he asks, leaning against the counter on his elbows. My heart accelerates at his question. He actually sounds intrigued, not disgusted, which is what I always expect.

"Something like that. But for me it's the stalking and the being unknown that I like. Well, at first."

"Wait a minute," Thomas says, standing up straight. "Does this mean you've done this before?"

Jayden grabs the bottle of whiskey from in front of Thomas and pours more into his glass. He's heard all of this previously, since we've spoken in length about my proclivity toward sex. He pulls one of the bar stools around to where he is and sits down, and Thomas does the same. I stay standing because my restlessness right now won't allow me to sit still. Taking a deep breath, I attempt to settle my nerves. Ready to put everything on the table.

"Whatever is said or done here at this cabin stays here. You have to promise. Swear it," I reiterate to make myself completely clear. Thomas nods, and Jayden leans back in the stool crossing his arms over his chest, waiting to hear everything all over again.

"Of course. I would never betray either of you. You know that," Thomas says as he leans his elbows on the counter, in anticipation to hear everything I have to say.

"Do you remember Vanessa?" I ask, and Thomas nods slowly. "Well, that was how we met. In an online kink chat room. We did that for a couple of months. That was until she told me she wanted more, so I ended it."

"So you broke up with your girlfriend–"

"She wasn't my girlfriend," I interrupt him. "We hooked up occasionally and hung out a little. But it was only about the sex. I didn't like her any further than that."

"Okay. So not your girlfriend, your fuck buddy. Whatever you want to call it. But you called it off because she... wanted a relationship?" He asks, trying to understand. I'm just thankful he doesn't seem to be judging me or calling me a sick and twisted asshole, which I would fully accept.

"Yeah. I was only hooking up with her because she was satisfying that itch. I mean, I have regular sex, albeit rough sex, but it doesn't do the same for me as chasing them down for it. I like the fight... the struggle. I don't know why, but I just do." And that's what it comes down to. I honestly can't explain exactly why it makes me harder than anything ever has. The begging and pleading. The tears and chase. That's what really gets my heart pumping and makes my dick harder than it ever has been.

Staring at Thomas as he processes everything I just said, I can tell he has questions on the tip of his tongue. Still, he seems reluctant, or scared, to ask me. But if we're going to get everything out, he might as well.

"Spit it out," I say on a heavy exhale, as I reach over,

pouring myself yet another glass of liquid courage I so desperately need right now.

"Look... I'm not judging, and I don't want to sound..." he releases a heavy breath. "I don't know, like an asshole. But isn't this basically... rape?" He asks with the last word almost whispered.

Now, this is what I'm used to. Giving Thomas a smirk, I know doesn't reach my eyes, I answer him. "No. That's where the consent comes into it. Girls enjoy being forced to submit, and some guys, like myself, like forcing it. The fight gets my blood pumping... the adrenaline flowing. It's almost like a high," I explain. "When I first researched this, I found it's more common than I expected or even knew. But, I don't go around telling people because I know I will be judged. I don't care what people think about me, but also, I don't feel it's anyone's business. Nor do I feel like explaining myself."

Thomas nods slowly and looks at Jayden. The silence that falls over the kitchen is deafening. All I can hear is the blood rushing in my ears and my heart beating in my chest.

"You knew about this?" he asks him, and Jayden nods.

"For quite a while, actually," he replies.

Thomas takes another minute to contemplate everything that was said, and he finishes off the last sip of his drink. He steps down from the stool and walks over to the sink, rinsing out his glass. This is the part that kills me. The waiting. Wondering if he is going to look back at me with disgust in his eyes and judgement in his words. Setting the glass in the dishwasher and closing it, he turns to face us leaning on the counter by the sink. I can tell he's contemplating his words right now. Letting everything that was said permeate in his mind. Finally, Thomas looks up and into my eyes.

"I appreciate you trusting me with this, Ky. And I won't break your trust. You have my word," he says.

"Thanks, T," I say with a release of my held breath and a nod of my head. Leaning on the granite top with my hands clasped, I inhale deeply. "Now, tomorrow's part might be a little more tricky and a lot more risky since it's outside. I'm going to need you both on high alert for her," I say, looking between them. "You remember the plan, right?"

They both nod.

"Good. Let's get some sleep. We're definitely going to need it," I say, knowing damn well I won't be sleeping in anticipation for tomorrow.

12

JAYDEN

We gather downstairs for breakfast after what I can only describe as a very restless night. My mind kept envisioning everything that Kyler said went down between them. It wasn't exactly jealousy but more impatience for my time with her. I let Kyler have his chance, now it's my turn. Well... our turn now. We tested her for the first time to see how she would react and if she would tell.

We each pitched in for some part of getting breakfast ready. Kyler made the coffee and prepared the orange juice, Thomas made the toast, and I set the table while Sky made the eggs and sausage. We left the cooking to her, since she loves that part and she's so good at it too. We all know if any of us guys tried, we would probably burn the cabin down.

Sitting down to finally eat, she seems a little better today from how Thomas said she appeared last night when we got back from the store. She keeps her eyes down on her plate except for the occasional glance my way. She looks like she wants to say something, but is still hesitant. I'm wondering if after todays excursion, maybe I will pull her to the side and see if she will confide in me.

Kyler is keeping his head down as he eats. I'm sure he's just trying to get into the right headspace. At least, that's what he's told me in the past. The room is too quiet, so I decide now is the time to bring up today's activity.

"So," I say wiping my mouth. "I was thinking about playing around in the woods today. Maybe a game of Capture the Flag with two teams. What do you think?" I ask, looking over at Skylan. She looks back at me but her eyes flit to Thomas and Kyler as well. My eyes never move from hers though. She seems a little skeptical.

Her eyes seem to linger on Kyler a little longer than normal, making me glance back at my best friend. He's still staring down at his plate, pushing the rest of his food around on his plate with a scowl on his face.

"That sounds like fun," Thomas says getting her attention off of Kyler, making me look back over at her. "Wanna be on my team, Butterfly?" he asks, flashing his eyebrows at her, making her giggle. That is one thing I am thankful for bringing Thomas in for. He's always great at distracting her and lifting her spirits. The guy can be walking sunshine.

He nudges her with his shoulder making her laugh even more. "Come on, you know you want to," he says.

Shaking her head, as she still laughs. "Sure."

Thomas laughs, fist pumping the air. "Hell yeah. You guys are gonna lose. Big time," he says, pointing at me and Kyler. He holds his hand up for Sky to give him a high five, which she does with an adorable tinkling laugh making me smile.

I feel Kyler stand next to me, gathering his plate and glass. "We'll see who wins," Kyler says, with a dark, mischievous smirk on his lips, making me smile as well.

A little over an hour later, after the kitchen is cleaned, we're all getting ready for the game in the woods. I'm standing at the bottom of the stairs, sliding my winter jacket on and zipping it up to hide what's beneath it. Kyler is doing the same as we wait for Thomas and Skylan to come downstairs from getting dressed.

"I hope T understands just how this needs to go. The timing on this is crucial," Kyler says in a gruff whisper, staring up the stairs.

"Yeah, he gets it. Stop doubting him. He's taken everything we've told him in stride. He's with us. If you can't trust him, trust me," I say, looking over at him. At my words he finally looks back at me nodding.

"This part is going to be difficult out there. Especially with how fucking cold it is," Kyler says, pulling on his beanie. "You got your mask?"

I nod and tap the front side of my jacket, indicating my inside pocket, making him nod.

"I just hope–" I start to say, before I hear Skylan's laugh echoing down the stairs. We both look up to see Thomas walking down the stairs with his arm draped over her shoulders. I hear a low growl coming from Kyler and take a quick glance over at him. His face is dark with fury, but I smile. He needs to learn to rein that jealousy in if we plan to do this together.

I glance back to Thomas and Skylan as they reach the bottom of the stairs. Looking her up and down, I see she's wearing pink joggers and a hoodie sweatshirt that looks like it belongs to me. I've heard a few of the guys on the team talk about how they feel when their girlfriends wear their jerseys or their clothes, and I never understood it until now. Seeing her in my sweatshirt does something to my ego and my cock. Knowing it's my clothes that will help to keep her warm while out there, makes me feel almost... proud.

Thomas eyes Kyler and notices the anger and jealousy rolling off him in waves. Hell, the outrage Ky is exuding is palpable. Their eyes lock and Thomas gives him a devious smirk, as he tightens his arm around Skylans neck, pulling her even closer to him and kissing the top of her head. Thomas is playing a dangerous game right now, but he knows what he's doing.

"You guys ready to lose?" Thomas asks laughing. Kyler turns to the table, snatching up the two yellow shirts we're using as flags.

"We've been waiting on you, asshole," he grunts out as he throws one of the shirts in Thomas's face, making him laugh. Kyler turns, opening the door and walking outside in huff. I laugh, but when I look over at Skylan, her face is downcast. Shaking my head, I grab her heavy jacket from the hook on the wall and walk over to her. Thomas removes his arm from around her neck, as I help her with her jacket. He goes to put on his own heavy jacket to give us a little moment of space.

"Don't mind Kyler. He's just being an ass," I lean in, whispering into her ear. With her coat on, I help her with her zipper. I enjoy helping to take care of her. I've always done this with her since she was little, but now it just means a little more to me that she allows me to continue to do this.

"We're supposed to be having fun, Jay. Why does he always act like this with me? Maybe I should just stay inside," she says glancing back up the stairs.

"Nope. You're coming out to play, too. While he and I are walking, I will talk to him about his attitude, okay?" I say, placing two fingers under her chin and lifting her face to mine. The way she looks back at me, she really has no idea what she does to me.

When she finally gives me a small nod with her smile, I smile back. Thomas walks up beside us as he zips his jacket. "Yeah, fuck him. Let's win this, Butterfly," Thomas says, grabbing the sleeve of her jacket, pulling her toward the door. This livens her up a bit making her laugh.

"We'll see who wins, asshole," I laugh, as we walk out, closing the door behind us.

Kyler and I have been walking for a bit, trying to stay far enough behind Sky and Thomas that we keep them in our sights yet they can't tell we're following them. We crouch behind a large boulder watching as they enter a little cave, just like we had discussed our first night here. Kyler's eyes are zeroed in on the mouth of the cave, and I nudge him with my elbow. His gaze does waver yet he still acknowledges me with a quiet, "Yeah?"

"Dude, you need to chill the fuck out about Thomas. I asked if you would be okay with him being included," I say in a hushed voice.

Once they are completely out of sight, disappeared into the darkness of the cave, he exhales harshly, shaking his head and finally looks over at me. Quirking an eyebrow at him, I wait for him to answer my silent question.

"Fuck," he whispers. "I know. And I am okay with it. It's just..." he shakes his head again, trying to process his thoughts. Finally looking me in the eyes, he finishes. "I've seen how they are together. They're already friends and... I just wish I could offer her that. I want it where it's effortless like that, you know?"

"You can, Ky. You just got to stop being such an asshole around her. She thinks you hate her."

His eyes shoot up to meet mine. "Seriously?"

I chuckle at his incredulousness. "Yeah, seriously. You're always such a dick around her." I shrug a bit, looking away from him back to the cavern. "Probably doesn't help that whenever the guys are over, I'm an asshole too."

Kyler starts to chuckle, which makes me laugh as well. Soon enough, I see Thomas coming to the mouth of the cave again, but his back is to us looking back inside the cave. I'm assuming he's talking to Skylan.

Reaching inside my jacket, I grab my mask and see Kyler doing the same. My mask looks just like his, but has red illumination instead of his white. I wanted to get them all the same, but distinguishing colors, when I grabbed them from the party store back home. Sliding our masks on, we remove our winter jackets and pull the hoods to our black sweatshirts up over our heads covering our hair. We look at each other.

"Here we go," Kyler says, with his voice altered, making me nod.

13

SKYLAN

"Look over there, Butterfly," Thomas says, pointing out a very large rock structure leading up to part of the forest as well. Trees grow tall over the formation along with bright green moss and other plants that seem to be thriving on it. The face of the wall has a large dark hole opening with greenery growing out of the rock obscuring the majoring of it from view. I look at it and then back to him skeptically. "Come on. This is the perfect place to hide our flag. They'll never find us in here," he says, grabbing my hand and pulling me behind him, as I reluctantly follow.

We've been walking around the woods looking for a spot to hunker down and hide until we are ready. This is just like a glorified hide and seek. I'm just glad they are including me in the fun and spending time with Thomas is always a bonus.

We walk through the entrance and the hollowed out area is larger than it looks from the outside but you can tell not many people have been in here. There are leaves and branches that have blown in the front and a large flat topped rock near the back corner. The rock doesn't seem man-made, just part of its structure.

Looking all around taking everything in, I'm still holding Thomas' hand as we make our way to the very back of the cavern. "At least it's not windy in here," I say.

Thomas lays the shirt that we're using as the flag on the top of the flat rock. "You can sit here."

I turn around and sit on the bright yellow shirt. Crossing my arms over my chest, trying to keep myself warm, I look up at him. Thomas stands in front of me and begins rubbing my upper arms, in an attempt to warm me up a bit. My cheeks heat up from his contact, and I just hope he thinks the blush on my cheeks is from the cold wind, not just from his touch alone. Thomas and I are friends, and don't want to let on that I have feelings for him. I'm too scared I will lose his friendship since he doesn't feel the same.

"I need to see if I can find where they are hiding their flag. I'm going to go scout around for a few minutes," he says, still rubbing my arms.

"Um... okay. I mean at least it's not windy in here," I say, trying to hide the fear in my voice. I'm not scared of being alone here, but I am a bit worried about getting lost if he doesn't come back right away.

The sides of Thomas' lips curl up in a crooked, sexy smile. Reaching up, he adjusts my beanie over my ears to cover them. "Don't worry. I won't be long," he says, as if he's reading my mind. "And as soon as we win this thing, we can get back to the cabin and build a nice fire and maybe watch a movie or something."

Smiling back at him and nodding, I ask, "Can we make s'mores?"

"Absolutely," he says, chuckling. Backing away toward the mouth of the cave, he keeps his eyes on me. "Now stay here, okay. Jayden will have my ass if you get lost in these woods alone," he says with a little laugh, making me smile and blush all over again. Thomas knows me too well.

Wrapping my own arms around me, I continue the ministrations of rubbing my upper arms trying to keep that warm feeling that he left and I nod. "I'm not going anywhere. With my sense of direction, I would end up in Timbuktu," I say as I settle myself on the hardened stone even more. We laugh together as he walks around the corner and out of sight.

I'm left alone with only my heavy breathing and the wind rustling the trees outside the cavern to keep me company. More leaves blow into the empty area through the opening from the wind blowing outside. The rock I'm sitting on is cold, sending another chill throughout my body but my ass seems to be warming it up pretty quickly. Cupping my hands in front of my mouth, I breathe into them trying to warm them up more. In an attempt to keep from shivering, I bring my knees further up to my chest and circle my arms around them. It's cold outside, but not too bad. Our winters here have been worse in the past and I'm accustomed to the weather and the snow from our many trips here.

The snapping of a twig outside the cave opening grabs my attention and halts my breathing. My head snaps in the direction of the noise. I'm praying it's just Thomas and that the scary guy from last night isn't roaming these woods. I don't think that he would even think to find me here out in the woods, so my mind rests slightly.

"Thomas?" I whisper loudly. I don't want to raise my voice too loud, in case it's not him. When no one answers, my head starts spinning again. The thought of the intruder from last night comes rushing to the forefront of my mind.

That crazy inner turmoil begins all over again like it did last night – worry and intrigue. Wondering what else he could and would do to me.

My head starts to reel with insane thoughts and revelations, when another snap of a twig and rustling of leaves is heard once again. I know bears and bobcats are in these woods because we've seen them before around our property. Now, my heart is racing, not knowing what is out there.

Oh, please let that be Thomas, I think as I slowly lower my legs from the rock and move to stand as quietly as possible. Moving further back against the cave wall, I place the flat top rock between me and whatever is out there. Movement again catches my eye as a tall, dark figure moves into view at the opening on the right coming from around the corner.

I audibly gasp and jump back bumping my head into the wall. I recognize that mask. He's wearing the same one he did last night, and he's dressed the same. Covered head to foot in all black with a hooded sweatshirt covering his head, gloves covering his hands, the edges of the illuminated mask have white X's for eyes and that intimidating smile that mocks my fear.

Unable to move, my eyes widen as I watch him still standing just inside the opening, my only exit from this hole in the mountain. Neither of us move. The time seems to stand still as my heart pounds and my breathing escalates to an embarrassing audible sound. I honestly don't know what to think about how my body reacts to this dark stranger. We seem to be in a stand-off, until another tall figure moves slowly into view from the other side of the entrance. Fuck, now there are two of them. I'm fucking terrified. If one wasn't enough, two of them will most definitely overpower me.

"No," I breathe out, my voice rough and shaky as my

head moves back and forth. My heart is racing, trying to beat out of my chest right now. I fear they can hear my heavy breathing and heart beating all the way over there.

The other guy is dressed almost exactly the same, hoodie, dark jeans, gloves and all, except his mask has red illuminated lights for the face. I'm shaking all over, but I don't know if it's from the thrill of things or pure unadulterated terror. My thighs automatically clench together as the fear and anxiety sky-rockets my libido for some insane reason. The cold around me seems to subside with how the adrenaline, fear and excitement run through my veins.

"M-my brother and his friends will be r-right b-back," I stutter out, trying to press myself even further against the hard rock walls. The rough stone scratches at my back as I try to shift myself even further behind the flat top rock. My hands press against the stone behind me trying to steady myself as my head runs through so many scenarios that equally terrify and turn me on.

A low, gravelly chuckle reaches my ears and I can't tell which one of these masked men are mocking me. As the one in the red mask looks over at his friend, the one with the white mask never takes his eyes off me as he shakes his head. When they are both once again focused solely on me, they take calculating steps forward. The way they approach me ensures I have nowhere to run.

As they near, I can tell that the one with the white mask is much larger in both height and muscle mass. As they make their way closer to where I'm standing, they begin removing their gloves slowly. Placing them in the front pockets of their hoodies, the one with the white mask reaches into his back pocket and pulls something out, and with a *snick*, the gleam of silver from a switchblade is seen in his right hand.

My eyes flicker quickly between his mask, the knife and the other guy. With me standing behind the boulder, they both approach from either side of it, effectively blocking me in. As they near, the one in the red mask then reaches into the front pocket of his hoodie, and my breath hitches at the cloth object in his hands now.

He opens it and holds it between both hands, fondling the material in a taunting fashion. I want to scream. Yell for Thomas, or my brother but my voice is caught in my throat at the intimidating figures before me. My blood is rushing in my ears and I'm scared to the point of being immovable. Not only at how large these two are but also the knife in the larger one's hand.

The larger of the two, with the white mask, moves closer to me, ensuring my focus stays on him. Since he's the one actually holding a weapon, it's difficult not to. Even though my heart is beating erratically, my focus stays on the mask of this formidable stranger. The fear of the unknown is there, but the war internally of me also being so insanely turned on is just confusing the hell out of me.

The hand, not holding the blade, comes up and cups my cheek. When I cringe away, the other hand with the knife comes up to rest against my jaw as he chuckles. His voice is still altered by some machine giving it an even more terrifying sound. Fear once again has me standing stock still besides the involuntary shaking my entire body is doing.

He moves to press up against my body, making me take an instinctive step back. When I move to step again, my back hits something hard and I realize I have run directly into the other daunting figure. I audibly gasp but still very much aware of the blade sitting against my face. The one behind me brings his hand up, knocking my beanie off my head while tangling my hair in his fist. Raising my hands to where he's roughly holding me, he gives it a harsh tug. The noise coming from my throat was a mixture between a squeak and a moan, making them both laugh.

Tears sting the back of my eyes and soon begin to streak my face. The menacing figure in front of me, wearing the white mask, leans down closer to my face. His head tilting to the side as he watches me cry. It seems to fascinate him. "Fuck, your tears turn me on. I want to see how much I can make you cry while you choke on my cock," he growls out. The voice distorter chills me to my bones along with the filthy words he says. The one behind me laughs.

The fear and arousal coursing through my body has me on edge. I feel like a freak, but having the sole focus of these intimidating and menacing men on me right now has me enraptured. It's a deep desire I have never told anyone about.

"Don't act like you don't want this," the second one behind me whispers in my ear. His voice altered in the same way as the first guy. I can feel the scrape of the plastic against the side of my face and my ear, making me shiver.

Trying to shake my head, which is difficult with his tight hold, I try to plead with them. "Please... please don't d-do this."

The hand cupping my face moves to encircle my throat. He doesn't squeeze hard enough to take away my air, but just enough to exert his dominance and let me know that they are in charge. Both of these men envelop my senses and make me even forget why I'm in this cave to begin with and what I came out here to do.

The white masked man gives a little nod to the one behind me and the hand in my hair disappears, but his body doesn't move from behind me. When his hand pulls away from my hair, my hands dropped to grip the forearm of the hand holding firmly to my neck. Before I can get a good hold on it, my arms are wrenched behind me. Another small squeak escapes my throat as they are secured in a cloth binding behind my back tightly. Now, my fear is ratcheted up tenfold, which only seems to increase my arousal even more so. *God, I'm so fucked up in the head.*

"Now, be a good little whore," the stranger behind me growls in my ear, the altered voice sending chills down my spine making my thighs clench together. "Don't cause any problems and you may enjoy this." He releases my bound arms, however, they are tied so tight I couldn't move them if I wanted to. My head is shaking unconsciously now as much as it can with him still holding my neck.

As I stare up at the stranger in front of me, his head tilts again studying me. I wish I could see his eyes but the illuminated x's give a glow to his irises and all I barely see is the shape. My mouth drops open, my tongue is tied and my throat dry, as another cloth is gently placed over my eyes from behind me once again. I'm panting. From fear or arousal, I don't know. It could be either or both at this point.

I'm terrified yet this is all my fantasies come true. Like they've been reading my journal or my mind. Or hell... been checking my kindle or book shelf. Who the fuck knows.

"Y-you don't want–"

"Oh, yeah, we do," one of them interrupts me. The hand around my throat drops away, but is quickly replaced with one from the guy behind me. Pulling me flush against his body with my back to his front, I feel his other hand move to grip my hip with his fingers skimming the bare skin under my jacket and hoodie, making me shiver involuntarily. At least I could blame the shiver on the weather, and not the fact that his strong hands feel amazing on my skin.

My mind begins to wonder how both of their strong

hands would feel all over my body, worshiping every inch of skin they touch. And as much as I would love to lose my virginity, this isn't the way I had thought of. And it definitely isn't who I want to give that to. But the thrill of the thoughts running through my head, makes me even wetter.

Pulling on the front of my joggers, the white mask guy dips his hand inside them and under my lace panties. I feel his large, warm hand cup the entirety of my mound. I try to jerk away, but there is nowhere to go with the other guy pressed up against my back. His hand is soft at first, then he begins to rub back and forth letting his touch become rougher. When his middle finger slides effortlessly through my slit, I try to close my thighs.

"Ah ah ah... I thought I told you not to give us any trouble," he says as he kicks my legs out wide making my whole body jerk. If I wasn't being practically held up by the stranger behind me, I probably would have fallen. My body leans back against the guy behind me and my head falls back against his toned and muscular chest. I bite my lip, trying not to moan out loud as his middle finger dips in through my wetness, rubbing roughly over my clit making it increasingly difficult not to vocalize my heightened state of arousal.

"Fuck. You're so wet for me... for us. You can't tell me you don't want this," the stranger in front growls. Kicking my feet further apart, he steps closer, throwing me off balance. Leaning against the masked man in the back even more, I feel his erection through his dark jeans, and fuck, he feels big as he presses it up against my lower back.

"Pl-please–" I try to speak before the hand around my throat tightens, restricting my voice and making me sputter. Stretching my neck even further, trying to get air, I hear him laugh as he leans closer to my ear. I can feel the plastic of his mask rub against my shivering, cold skin, just making me warm all over which is an even more contradictory feeling.

"Now, now, little whore. There's no need to beg. We plan on making all those filthy little dreams come true," the stranger in the back says, making me whimper. Shaking my head in a pathetic response to try and deny what I know is the truth, but there is no way in hell that they know or that I will admit this to them.

One of the masked strangers slides their large hand under my jacket and sweatshirt and begins squeezing my breast. I hear the one in the front groan loudly as he tweaks my nipple. I don't even recognize the moans and sounds escaping my own lips. But the way my body is on fire from their hands on me, I've never felt this way before.

The sound of something hitting the cave floor makes me jump. It sounds like one of them dropped their mask. My pants are roughly pulled down my thighs but due to my shoes, they are not removed. The cold air envelops me until I feel hot breath on my most sensitive spot. I feel the coldness of the blade move up my outer thigh, and with the flick of a quick movement, he slices the side of my lace panties. Moving, I feel the same to the other and my panties are slowly pulled from my body.

Feeling the moisture of a wet tongue lapping at my pussy makes me gasp. "Oh, god," I exclaim. A dark chuckle comes from behind me, sending waves of chills from the cold air and the overwhelming pleasure all over me. The sound of the mask hitting the floor once again reaches my ears, and I'm guessing that since I'm blindfolded they have no worry about me identifying them.

Warm breath ghosts over my ear and a wet tongue licks up the side of my neck. When teeth nibble on the fleshy lobe of my ear, I drop my head to the side giving this delicious stranger more access. I feel and hear him growl as he continues to feast on my sensitive skin.

Callused hands grasp my thighs pushing them apart, and I just know I will be wearing bruises from this rough treatment. He can't stretch my legs too far, with my joggers down by my ankles, but he pushes them as far as they will go to open me up further.

His tongue circles my clit then two fingers are thrust inside of me, causing me to focus my thoughts on that, even though the stranger behind me hasn't stopped feasting on my neck or kneading my breasts. And with everything being done, I am in sensory overload and can feel an orgasm building.

My panting is getting louder as well the moans they are eliciting. "Please– fuck– oh, m-my– g–" I'm stumbling over my words. Not making any sense nor do I even know what I'm begging for. "Please... please... pl–" a loud moan interrupts my words. I still can't believe that it came from me, as my orgasm rips through me like a tornado, making them both chuckle.

Slumping against the stranger behind me, I can only hear my heavy breathing and the blood rushing in my ears. The one in front of me, begins to pull my pants back up into place as he stands. The one behind me gives me a gentle kiss just below ear, the gentleness out of place with what just happened. I hear rustling around and feel them move, before I feel the one in front of me step closer pressing into my body making me gasp.

"Open your mouth," he growls out. The distortion once again back, so I'm guessing the rustling sound was them putting their masks back on. Hesitating just a moment, I then do as he says. Slowly fingers are slid over my lips and tongue. A sweet, tangy flavor erupts on my taste buds.

"Suck," he orders. Closing my lips around the fingers, I do as I'm told, letting my tongue move against those callused digits.

From behind me, I hear him moan like he wishes it was him. "How do you taste?" he asks but with the fingers in my mouth, I can't answer.

"She tastes so fucking sweet. Better than any honey I've ever tasted," he says as he pulls his fingers from my mouth. As he slowly pulls them, they pull my bottom lip downs as he wipes the saliva and the remnants of my arousal over my chin.

Feeling the one from the front reach around the back of my head, he unties the blindfold, as the other one wraps his hand around my throat once again. I slowly blink my eyes open trying to see.

Looking up into the illuminated mask once again, I ask, "Why?"

He tilts his head as if my question confuses him. The fingers splayed out on my neck begin to move soothingly. Almost as if they are trying to calm my nerves and comfort me. I'm so fucking confused. All these conflicting feelings and actions.

"Why... me?" I ask again, and he just stares at me. It's like he's trying to convey his reasoning mentally and not wanting to verbalize it.

"Why not you?" he asks then steps back slightly. When the man behind me steps back, I stumble into the cave wall, not realizing how much he had been holding me up, especially with my hands still bound behind my back. After what felt like several minutes of the one in front of me staring me down, he turns and walks away.

My legs feeling weak from such an intense orgasm along with the adrenaline from everything that just happened, I slide down the wall to the cave floor. The one that had been behind me, with the red mask approaches me again. Tears are streaming down my face as he squats down beside me. As he releases the binding, I slowly bring my arms in front of me to massage my wrists trying to help with the blood flow. Looking down at them and away from his daunting mask, I see where the binding cinched into my skin. That's definitely going to bruise, I'm sure of it.

With the cloth that had once held my wrists together gathering into one hand, he places his elbows on his knees and looks at me in bewilderment. His hands are playing with the cloth that was just around my wrists. I can tell he's scrutinizing my face as we sit in silence.

"Admit it," his gruff altered voice says. Focusing on massaging the feeling back into my wrists and hands, I still don't look at him. I'm embarrassed by my reaction to this entire ordeal and scared that he will see it in my eyes. The fact that I came and my body enjoyed it as much as it did. I can try to convince myself that it is just my body, but I know it is something I have always wanted. Something I crave, even more so now that I have experienced a morsel of what I have read in my books.

Two fingers are placed under my chin, making my eyes immediately close as my face is lifted. Tears are streaming down my face as I hesitantly open my eyes to look into the mask.

"Admit it," he repeats in a harsher, more commanding voice.

My voice is as soft as a whisper. "Admit what?" I ask, confused.

His thumb comes up softly moving across my bottom lip then pulling it down slightly. "Admit you wanted this," he says, and my breath hitches. It's like he's in my damn head. I move to shake my head, but I hear him tsk. "Don't lie. Not to me and not to yourself."

My mouth drops open slightly as a gush of air leaves my lungs. My eyes fall away from the mask to the ground, unable to look directly at him. I feel my face heat up with the blush of embarrassment. Why does he need me to admit it? What satisfaction will he get from hearing my admission?

"Admit. It," he grinds loudly, and the sound startles me to look back into his mask. My brow furrows because now he's making me angry.

"Why?" I sound a little bolder than before. "Why do you need me to admit it? To set your conscience at ease? Fuck you," I hiss the last words out with venom lacing my tone.

I hear his deep chuckle from behind the mask as he shakes his head slowly. He releases my chin and stands to his full height, forcing me to crane my neck to look up at him from my place still on the ground. The black holes where his eyes should be peer down at me.

"I want you to realize it... and admit it to yourself that you want it. So next time... you can enjoy it that much more," he says and turns, walking to the cave entrance. What he said just hits me. *Next time?*

"N-next time?" I question, scooting back further into the cave. He stops but doesn't turn around. I notice the other stranger standing just inside the mouth of the cave with his massive arms crossed over his chest, watching our interaction.

"Next time, sw–" he stops himself but quickly recovers. "Next time, we won't be so gentle."

He walks quickly out of the cave and around the corner out of sight. The one in the white mask doesn't take his eyes off of me. He stands there stoically for a few seconds until I look away. From my peripheral I can see him leave as well.

My skin is on fire. I can still feel their hands all over me. My tears have dried up, because the masked stranger is correct. I have wanted this. Do want this. This is precisely what I have been wanting for a while now. Something I have talked to Bri about, and not just in passing but in great depth.

After a few moments of going over everything in my head, I listen to make sure I don't hear them anymore. Slowly I stand up, brushing my pants off of the dirt. Glancing around, I look for my panties that were cut off of me but they are nowhere to be found. Quietly I move to the front of the cave, scooting along the wall, trying not to make any noise and still listen out if they come back.

Once I'm at the mouth of the cave, I notice the breeze blowing a little more making it colder out in the open. Glancing around the corners, I don't see any trace of them. I know I can't stay here. They could be back at any time. They could be just acting like they left. But I know I'm not safe here. Looking around the left and then right of the edge of the cave, I don't see anything. The snow is falling even more now. *Where the fuck is Thomas?*

14

KYLER

Jayden and I crouch down behind the boulder where we originally watched Thomas and Skylan enter. Nerves are shot right now but the adrenaline pumping through my veins keep me on my toes. The electric current beneath my skin is moving like a livewire, keeping me grounded yet still antsy. My eyes stay hyperfocused on the mouth of the cave just waiting to see what she does. I hear the leaves rustle softly nearby, but I don't lose my concentration on my center of attention. Jayden removes his mask, resting it on top of his head and turns his head to the noise behind us. Slowly, I do the same as I slide my mask up to sit on the top of my head as well, so I can see better.

My hands are itching to touch her again. Her taste still lingers on my tongue. She reacted just like I expected. She's going to look even more beautiful, completely wrecked under me, begging us to make her ours.

"So..." I hear Thomas whisper behind me. "How did it go?" he asks.

Jayden takes a deep breath and releases it slowly. "Ky

was right. I could see it in how she reacted to everything," he says on a whispered breath.

"What now?" Thomas asks. Glancing his way quickly then back to where my focus needs to be. They are both looking to me for our next move. A sly devious smirk lifts one side of my mouth as I see Skylan peek her pretty little head out of the side of the cave.

"Now..." I growl out as I lower my mask once again. "Now we have a little fun doing exactly what our little beauty wants us to do," my voice altered once again in a low rumble. Turning to look at Jayden and Thomas, they both nod at me. They both slide their masks on. Jayden brings his red illuminated mask down from where it had been resting on top of his head and Thomas pulls the blue illuminated mask from inside his jacket.

Thomas removes his heavy winter jacket, sitting it next to ours behind the boulder. I hear a snap of twig and my head whips back around to see Skylan moving around the large tree sitting just outside the cave she was hiding in. She's looking around like she's expecting us to just jump out and grab her. Little does she know, we plan to do more than that. Soon we will not only make her ours but show her exactly who owns her... mind, body and soul. Bringing her most darkest desires and fantasies into her reality. We will have her constantly dripping in pleasure, she will never want for anyone or anything else.

With my sole focus on our little whore, I watch as she flips both of her hoods up over her head then zips her winter jacket back up. She's crouching low, trying to watch in every direction and even glancing over her shoulder. Heading off in the direction toward the cabin, Skylan attempts to stay low and it seems as quiet as possible.

"You remember the plan. Let's split up and get her into

the cabin," I growl out as I stand to my full height. "As much as I would love to fuck her out here in these woods, I want to take our time with her and out here in the freezing cold and snow, isn't the best way." Taking a step around Jayden and Thomas, I move to start in the direction she headed. I hear them quickly discussing which way they are going as I quickly follow behind our little beauty.

Keeping my full attention on the beauty a ways in front of me, I keep moving as quietly but as quickly as possible. She's too busy looking around her and not focusing on what is directly behind her. I'm far enough back that I'm sure she can't hear my footsteps over the sound of her own along with what I'm sure is her pounding heart right now.

Thomas and Jayden move in opposite directions on either side of her to make sure she doesn't stray too far from the path that was covered in snow since we've been out in these woods. Our little beauty has a tendency to get lost easily, so we are just making sure she gets back into the cabin where it's nice and cozy for what we have planned.

My steps quicken the closer to the cabin we get. It's time to get her heart racing and blood pumping even more now. I want her soaking wet for us.

The sound of a branch snapping ricochets off to my right, and Skylan freezes ducking down toward the ground looking that way. Closer than what I expected, the lights to Jayden's mask illuminate as he stands there looking fiercely intimidating. He's not moving, just staring at her.

Her gasp can be heard in the quietness of the woods. She stands quickly but I'm guessing since he's not moving, she isn't either. I wonder to myself if he did that on purpose now, making me quietly chuckle. Her head shifts looking in the direction of the cabin. The smoke from the fireplace can be seen from here so she knows which way to run now.

Another snap of twig even closer behind her makes her whip her head around once again. I'm still moving slowly and noiselessly forward toward her. Thomas turns his blue mask lights on and he is even closer than Jayden is. Her head is shaking minutely, but still visibly. We now have her surrounded. I am now the closest to her, so I then step on a branch making my presence known.

Skylan jumps all over turning to face me. I can see the fear in her face as I stand there staring down at her. I wonder if she can put it together that it's us. Hoping she doesn't but I know how smart our little beauty is, that she has to be questioning it at the very least. Flipping the switch in my hand, I illuminate my white mask.

"No... how... how many are there?" she asks quietly. It sounds like she's talking to herself. Jayden and Thomas still don't move, but when I take a step forward, she mimics my movement stepping back. Tilting my head to one side, watching her closely, I see her eyes flit from side to side making sure they still haven't moved.

Before I can take another step, she turns to run, making me laugh loudly. "Run, little whore. If you think you can escape all of us," I yell through the voice alterer in my mask. This time, she doesn't even falter. She runs straight for the cabin, not looking behind her. I'm sure she thinks she will be safe in there. Where does she think we, meaning myself, Jayden and Thomas, are? Is her fear ratcheted up so high that she's not even thinking straight?

We move slowly through the woods. Our plan isn't to chase after her out here. It was to make her think we were going to chase her. We can plan a real chase out here later after she knows who she's dealing with. The elements are too harsh right now and I don't want her to seriously get hurt or sick.

As we converge on the path to the cabin, I can see them glance at me but my eyes don't leave her. I need to make sure she doesn't trip or hurt herself. We pick up our pace to make sure she knows we're still behind her. None of us are trying to be quiet now.

When she breaks the forest's edge into the small back-yard of the cabin, she trips over something falling to the ground. She finally takes that moment to glance behind her and see us heading directly toward her. Her brow furrows as I watch her eyes flit from each of us contemplating something.

Is she considering the thought it could be us? Is she questioning the possibility that the three masked men chasing her could be her brother and his two best friends? Before I can get a read on what exactly is going on behind her beautiful brown eyes, she scrambles to her feet, sprinting to the heavy back door.

Throwing herself against the door, it doesn't move. In her haste she is unable to get a tight enough grip on the knob to open it. Finally, the door flies open making her stumble inside, falling to the tile floor of the kitchen. She scrambles backward, on her hands and knees, throwing the door closed.

"Jay," I instruct quietly, making him turn his head toward me. "Go through the front." He nods solemnly, stalking noiselessly around the front of the cabin to the main door that we purposely left unlocked. "T," I say turning my attention to someone other than her. "Go to the side. The basement door is unlocked," I say and he nods, jogging over in the opposite direction as I continue walking up to the back door.

Looking in through the sheer curtained window, I see that the kitchen is empty. I reach for the door knob and attempt to turn it but it's locked. At least she tried to keep us out. My hand deftly enters into my front jeans pocket, pulling out the spare keys that Jayden had given me last night while we planned this. The adrenaline running through my entire system, I don't even feel the cold breeze the way I should.

Slowly I push the key into the slot and turn, hearing the quiet snick of the lock disengaging. As quietly as I can, I slide through the partially opened door. My eyes dart all around the vast kitchen area, trying to figure out where she's hiding.

The deadbolt above the knob is a key lock and open mechanism, only a key will work in it. I move to lock it, ensuring she can't leave this way without a key. Jayden and I are the only two here with the keys, so she won't be leaving through this way for sure.

Once the kitchen door is locked up tight, I slide the keys back into the front pocket of my black jeans and turn to face the open kitchen area. Even with the daylight streaming in through the windows around the kitchen, there are still so many shadowed areas that she could be hiding. My head is swiveling back and forth, allowing my eyes to adjust to slight darkness. I don't move from in front of the door just yet.

Hearing the quiet click of the door in the front room, I know Jayden is in place. A smile lifts the side of my lips up, when I hear a soft gasp from the living area. I know then she didn't hear me come in, but either she heard Jayden or saw him. This is the end game now. What has happened before now, has been the appetizer. This... this is the main course and I plan to devour my little beauty.

15

SKYLAN

Three of them now. How the fuck do they keep multiplying? The large one in the white mask steps forward making me take an involuntary step backward. My eyes move from side to side trying to keep the other two in my peripheral vision. They aren't moving, but the large one is. Before he can make another move, I turn on my heel and sprint in the direction of the cabin.

If I can get there, I can lock them out. I left my phone upstairs and I'm hoping to all hell that one of the guys took their phones with them. I can call Jayden and tell him to come home. I can't tell him about what's happened, but as long as he's here I will be safe. He may be an asshole, but he always makes me feel safe.

"Run, little whore. If you think you can escape all of us," I hear his dark voice behind me. Fuck! I can hear in the threat just exactly what they plan to do to me. And I'm so fucked in the head that I'm excited about it. My blood is pumping in fear and arousal. Surely my panties are soaked. Oh wait... I don't have any on because they stole them.

Feeling the snow and ground crunch under my feet, the

wind whips around my face making my cheeks and nose feel numb but I still run as hard and fast as I can. As cold as it is, I'm sweating from all of this exertion. My heart pounds and my breathing is stinging my chest from the cold.

Pushing even harder, I can see the break in the trees. As soon as I step through them, my feet stumble over a fallen branch. I hit the ground hard, but can't stop now. I can feel the scrapes on my hands and knees, but I quickly recover and scramble back up on my feet running again. I can't even take a moment to look back. My attention solely focused on the kitchen door.

Ramming into the door from running full speed, the door rattles. I grab the knob, shake the door, twisting it but my hand slips over it. I can't get a grasp on it. I shake the door, scared it's locked. Trying once more gripping the aluminum knob harder, I throw it open falling inside to the tile floor.

Flopping over I kick the door closed then scramble quickly to lock it. Reaching to where the deadbolt key should be, it's gone. My blood runs cold. I'm seriously hoping Jayden took it the other night when they left to go to the store, and it wasn't the masked invader.

Moving on my hands and knees, I crawl quickly out of the kitchen just around the corner. I'm hidden next to my mom's bookcase, crouched down. Covering my mouth with both hands trying to control my breathing so they can't hear me. I need to rest just a moment before I try to run upstairs.

Taking a deep breath and releasing it slowly, I look down at my scraped palms and then see the dirt patches on my joggers. My knees are burning and my hands are throbbing. Glancing around, I listen to the quiet house. Maybe they left. Just gave up.

Pushing myself up from my hiding spot, I want to make a

run to mine and Jayden's bathroom. It's the most secure of the house besides the basement, plus I need my phone to call my brother. But before I can fully stand I hear the front door open. The gentle creak of the hinges is unmistakable, so I drop back down and push myself as far as I can in the corner. Hoping it's one of the guys, I peek around where I'm sunk down. I see the menacing one with the red mask walk through the door. He's so intimidating with his height and size. I can tell under those clothes, he's just as muscular as the large one. I gasp as I throw myself further back into the corner. Hoping to hell he didn't hear that, I cover my mouth trying to conceal my heavy breaths. Forcing my back against the wall between the corner and the bookshelf, I try to make myself disappear.

The shadow of the tall intruder comes closer to my position, making me shrink back. My heart is pounding and my breaths are coming in gasps. Lifting my eyes where the shadow is coming from, his entire focus is on me. Why is it, when I finally get a guys full attention, he's a maniac. My eyes grow wide as my head shakes back and forth. The red-masked man moves slowly toward my position.

My eyes flit in all directions. I don't want to take my focus off of him, but I need to assess my surroundings and make an escape plan. As my eyes move toward the back area, the door to the basement begins to open slowly. My breath hitches even more as the new blue-masked guy walks around the door. I can tell when he recognizes the other guy walking toward me and they both then focus on my little hiding place.

My heart is practically pounding out of my chest now. The adrenaline rush from the fear of what is to come and getting everything you want, is extremely unnerving. I don't know whether I should just enjoy the feeling or run like hell. Not only do I feel like a freak for this, the internal conflict is going to drive me insane.

From my position crouched on the floor, they move to stand above me just a few steps away. The way the one in the blue mask keeps glancing over to the other one, makes me wonder who is in charge of this, and do they have a leader. Speaking of leader, where is the other one. The one in the white mask.

The one in the red mask moves closer, squatting down just in front of me with his forearms resting on his thick thighs. His entire presence engulfs my senses. As my focus is on him, from the corner of my eye, I see movement and the largest one of them all, the one in the white mask, comes around the corner from the kitchen standing right next to me. He peers around the bookcase looking down at us as he leans his shoulder on the wood shelf. My breathing is heavy, and the conflict is even stronger now. They have me surrounded and all I can think of is what it's going to feel like to lose my virginity to one of these massive men.

And if the conflict inside of me isn't bad enough, the red-masked guy squat down in front of me reaches out, cupping my chin in his massive hand so very gently. I would have never guessed one of these muscular menacing men could have had such a soft touch. My body is vibrating from anxiety but my first instinct isn't to pull away, I want to enjoy it. It's touches like these that also makes me fall into a false sense of security with them. My body just wants to give into whatever it is they want.

"Are you ready to admit it?" he asks, lifting my face so that I'm looking directly at him. Tears well in my eyes and I try to shake my head. I still can't answer him. His gentle hold on my chin tightens as he tilts his head to the right.

If I admit that I want this... that I have been craving

this... I would be acknowledging how fucked up I am in the head. How depraved I am wanting something so wrong and depraved from all of my books.

Shaking his head, he clicks his tongue in disapproval. His hold on my chin tightens as he pulls my face closer to his. Feeling his breath ghost over my lips, I then look into the dark holes for his eyes. I can just make out the shape as they narrow on me. "Whether you admit it or not, this is happening," he says, brushing his thumb over the swell of my cheek. Releasing my face, he stands to his full height looking down on me. Craning my neck to look up at the tall figure standing in front of me, I shiver at his imposing stature as he speaks. "Before this is over, you're going to be begging us for more."

"Who... who are you? What do you want?" I ask with a shaky voice. He just shakes his head once again.

"What do we want?" he asks, ignoring the first part of my question then shifting his gaze from one accomplice to the other before they once again rest on me. I hear a dark chuckle, but don't know who it's coming from. The sounds of it reverberate throughout the room and down my spine making me shiver. "Everything... from you."

At his confession, my eyes widen and a small gasp leaves my lips. The one in the red mask takes a step back. With speed like no other, the intruder right beside me in the white mask strikes out like a snake reaching down to grab the hair at the base of my skull. Pulling me to my feet. As my hands fly to his corded forearms. He moves through the front living area. Choking on a scream, my legs move on their own accord just trying to keep up. He doesn't speak yet his silence is deafening.

As we move through the front area, I'm kicking and moving trying to get loose. His hold is like steel. I know already there is no chance of getting away. I see from the corner of my eye, he reaches into his pocket and pulls out the blade he had earlier. Even through the rushing blood in my ears, I still hear the quiet *snick* as he opens it. I suck in a harsh breath as he pulls me to a stop.

Pulling me by my hair to stand in front of him, he holds the blade against my cheek once again. He doesn't break the skin, but the threat is still very visible and abundantly loud. "Be. Still," he grits out. "Quit fighting it and you just might enjoy it."

We continue into the back family room area, and I see the one in the blue mask approach the one in the red as I am dragged by my hair by the largest and scariest of them all. Hearing the other two speak in heated voices, I can tell there is discourse in their ranks. The hand in my hair tightens, but I can tell by the way he's holding my hair, it probably could hurt worse. It was the shock of being lifted from my crouched position.

"Shut it," he growls loudly looking over his shoulder at his two companions. Their conversation comes to an abrupt halt. I'm thrown onto the oversized plush L-shaped couch in the main family room. A quick gust of air is pushed from my lungs when my chest hits the back and my knees hitting the cushions are sore from falling outside earlier.

Hair in my face, I'm terrified to move. I move both of my knees up onto the couch and slowly try to make myself as small as possible. "Secure her," the dark rumbling voice comes from behind me as the tall one moves back just a step.

Peering through my hair, I can see he hasn't taken his eyes off of me. The other two move up closer to me. "Remove her jackets first. I want a look at those perfect tits," he says and I can hear the smile in his altered voice.

A whimper escapes me as I wrap my arms around my body hoping to stem off their advances. I know it's useless. Just one of them can over power me... let alone all three. I can see in their motions the blue and red mask are deciding who will do his bidding as he takes a seat on the strong oak coffee table in the center of the room only a few steps from the couch I'm on. I guess he doesn't want to miss anything.

When the one in the blue mask sits down next to me, I jump slightly at his proximity not expecting him to sit next to me. He lifts his right hand slowly and pushes the hair from my face behind my ear. He's looking at me pensively. He runs his knuckles down the side of my face gently. The back of his knuckles softly moving over the front of my throat until his hand reaches the zipper of my large winter coat. His gentle nature confuses me, making my breath catch in my throat. He is so different from the other two. As the zipper lowers, he uses his other hand to pull my arms from around my center so he can fully remove it.

My entire focus is on him. His tender touch doesn't seem to compute in my head with what's actually going on. Them being in here uninvited and chasing me down in the woods. Once the zipper releases he pushes the jacket off my shoulders and the other guy helps to pull it off, throwing it onto the floor.

"I might be into delayed gratification... but this is fucking ridiculous," I hear the white masked invader mumble, before barking, "Hurry the fuck up!"

Even with the wicked words being spoken, I never take my focus off of the closest danger right now. I know he isnt' safe yet his gentleness is once again lulling me into a false sense of security. He reaches down to grab the hem of my hoodie, Jayden's hoodie. The one thing that has been really keeping me strong. Feeling him close by.

My hands move trying to keep that one piece of clothing still on. "No... please," I whisper, making him tilt his head inquisitively. My focus then shifts moving between them all. "You don't have to do this. If my brother and his friends come back... they will kill you."

I see the blue masked guy move back just slightly but the larger one, the one in the white mask, stands abruptly still holding the blade in his hand. Pointing the blade at my hoodie, he moves closer making the one in the red mask shift aside slightly to make room for him.

"If they come... they can enjoy the show," he says as he bends down. "Now remove it or I will cut it off of you."

16

JAYDEN

The fuck he will cut my hoodie off of her, over my dead body. That's her favorite. I stay stoically still though none-the-less, because I know it's an empty threat. Kyler knows why she's trying to hold onto that piece of clothing at the very least, and I know she won't allow it to happen and will remove it before it gets that far. He also knows how close she and I are. Keeping my head still, I move my eyes to look at Thomas. If anyone is going to break this or bring it to a screeching halt, it will be him. He's too nice of a guy, and really cares for Skylan, plus the argument we just got into a few moments ago, told me he wasn't going to let Kyler go much further.

Kyler begins walking toward the family room dragging Skylan behind him by her hair. Her fighting him is what is really causing the pain. Thomas's head is whipping between them and me. "What the actual fuck? You said he wouldn't hurt her," he growls as he shifts to remove his mask while moving to try to stop Kyler from going any further.

"Stop. Fucking stop, I said," I growl out grabbing his arm making him come to a halt as Kyler continues to drag her to the

other room. When I know they are out of ear shot, I speak directly to him in a low voice. "He's not hurting her. Not much more than what you've done to a couple of the cheerleaders during rough sex. I promise, I won't let it go much further," I say.

Thomas huffs out a breath of exasperation, gripping the back of his neck with both hands, taking a step back and looking down at the ground. Shaking his head, I can tell he's struggling with wanting her and also wanting to protect her. His insides are warring with each other.

Lifting my hand, I firmly grab his shoulder. "Just a little longer, T. Everything is within reach. She's going to be ours soon enough. Okay?" I ask my best friend, dipping my head a bit to try to look into the eyes of the mask. His eyes are anxious, but finally they focus on me. He takes a moment to let everything calm inside himself. Nodding his head and releasing a harsh breath, his hands drop to his sides and he looks back at me directly.

"Why does he have that knife?" he asks me. My brow furrows for a moment because I honestly don't have an answer for that. I wasn't prepared when he pulled that out in the cave let alone now. We never discussed the need of a weapon at all. We know we can overpower her without any of that.

"Don't worry. Kyler won't hurt her," I say. In my head I want to finish that with 'at least I don't think he will', but I don't say that part outloud. I just need to keep a closer eye on him. Kyler is taking this a little further than we originally spoke about. "Now, get your head on straight and let's go do this." Nodding his head, I drop my arm from his shoulder and we move to the family room when we see Kyler shove her onto the large, overstuffed couch.

Thomas is being so gentle with her, which lets me know he's going to be good for her. He will be the soft touch to Kyler's rough nature and my possessiveness. When Kyler speaks, I can physically see her shrink back. It's crazy that she still hasn't put two and two together, knowing it's us behind these masks. I'm sure it's because of the stress of it all. I'm hoping its relief we see in her eyes when we show her and not more fear. Fear that we could do this.

After only a few moment's she moves her hands to the bottom of the hoodie and lifts it over her head, dropping it next to herself. Her t-shirt comes off with it, so now she's just sitting there in her lace bra and joggers. After detangling her hand from inside my hoodie she attempts to cover her breasts, but Kyler isn't having any of that.

Kyler glances at Thomas, and even though Thomas's eyes haven't left her, he speaks to him. "Secure her," he growls through the voice enhanced mask. Thomas's head whips to look at Kyler. I can tell he wants to question him. Glancing at me, I give a small shake of my head. Imploring him to hold off just a little longer. I can see Sky glance up at Thomas with a pleading look. Thomas continues to look between Kyler and me, I give him a nod to do as Kyler asks. I hate that he has such an inner fight about this. This isn't the way he would have done any of this. Neither would I, but Kyler has always been a force to be reckoned with, plus at the time it seemed like a good idea.

How he approached this whole thing with me was very convincing. Hell, seeing how she reacted in the cave just supported his reasoning and it seemed like a hot idea to me. I'd always heard about primal play but never indulged in it. And while this little game has had my cock hard since we started it... I still have yet to have any relief. Which I'm hoping comes soon enough.

I meant what I said to Thomas. I'm not going to let this go on any longer. I would much rather she truly know who is chasing her rather than having the possibility of causing real damage to our relationship before I can even show her how I feel about her. It's also a huge pull to keep it a secret because I don't know how she's going to react when we finally reveal who we are.

Thomas reluctantly stands to walk around the back of the couch. Skylan's eyes track his movements. I can see the fear but also a hint of excitement in her eyes. When he rounds the back of the couch, she moves to get up. Kyler moves in front of her halting her attempt, forcing her to look up the entirety of his muscular body.

Thomas pulls out a cloth from his front hood pocket. Reaching around removing her hands that are still trying to hide her chest from us, he secures them behind her back.

"Sit back," Kyler commands in his darkest tone. Slowly she leans back against the cushions, but as her face twists up I can tell she's uncomfortable. Eyes glistening with apprehension, but no more tears falling. Kyler glances once again my way, nodding. I move and wrap the cloth in position around her eyes, blindfolding her once again.

My best friend uses his legs to separate her thighs, spreading her open a bit. Too bad she still has those damn joggers on. Kyler lifts the blade pressing the flat of the blade against her lips. Not very hard but enough to let her know it's there and it is most definitely a threat. Her lips open just slightly with a bit of a gasp. I can see the appeal of the knife now. That shiny silver against her tanned skin is erotic.

Wondering what exactly he has planned for this weapon, I need to make sure he doesn't take this too far. My step-sister isn't going to fight back but she's also not one to shy away either. Seeing the turmoil of slight nuances in eyes and her reactions have been such an eye opener for me. It's also put a bunch of other ideas in my head for the future... if there is a future for us.

The blade is slowly moved down her throat to her chest then even further to her flat stomach. I see Kyler watching where the knife trails over her tan skin. Her muscles jump where ever he touches her with it. I wonder if it's in fear, or is she ticklish there or possibly could it be the anticipation... expectations of what's to come.

"Pl-please... please don't do this," she cries quietly. Stepping up closer to peer over Kyler's shoulder down at where she's laid back on the couch. Thomas leans over watching the same thing, resting his forearms on the back of the couch. That twist is building in him. Worried Kyler is going to hurt her but also turned the fuck on just like me with how this is going. My stepsister is fucking gorgeous laid out like this.

"Are you ready to admit now?" I ask, making her head shift to the direction of mine, but she still doesn't answer. Her stubbornness shows no bounds. But I'm ready to get this game over and show her exactly who we are and what we can do.

I look at Kyler more now and his head swivels to meet my gaze. "Have you had enough?" I ask him. It's only when Skylan answers, we focus back on her not expecting her reply.

"Yes," she whimpers.

"Yes, what? Yes, you're ready to admit it, or yes, you've had enough?" Kyler grunts out.

She doesn't respond again. Releasing a heavy breath, she just shakes her head. From behind her, Thomas stands to his full height lifting his mask from his face resting it on top of his head. His hazel eyes look worried as they bounce between me and Kyler. He leans his hands on the back of the couch, dropping his head down looking at Skylan as she just lays there.

We discussed this already. We had our fun and filled one of her fantasies. And though we plan to continue this, if she wants of course, we don't want to take this too far right now. If we fuck her without her knowing it's us, it is venturing into the rape scenario and that's not how I want our first time to be.

"What do you want?" I ask quietly. She shakes her head again and gives a little sniffle. I'm sure if the blindfold wasn't there, she might be crying. My Skylan is gorgeous and no other girl can compare to her. Cannot even hold a candle to her. But crying... tears flowing down her face... she's fucking stunning. Now I just need her to look at me with those caramel colored eyes, then it will be perfect. But look at me... not this masked man.

Sitting down next to her on the couch, I lean close to her. She tries to shy away but the restrictions of her tied hands and how she's leaning back on the couch she can't move too much. I'm close enough to smell the slight scent of the mix of perfume and shampoo wafting from her. "Tell me," I encourage her, my breath softly ghosting over the shell of her ear. I see her slightly flinch from my new proximity.

"I-I don't know," she whispers.

"What if... we give you what we know you want," I say, but she stays quiet. All three of us guys stay quiet and unmoving. We've been waiting for her to admit that this is something she wants. We said as soon as she does admit it, we will reveal ourselves. Letting her know that all three of us want her bad enough to share her rather than her end up with just one of us.

"I don't know," she speaks so softly, that it's spoken on a breath. If I wasn't so in tune with her I wouldn't have heard it.

Glancing up at the maskless Thomas then we both look to Kyler. I slowly remove my mask, as does Kyler. I run my thumb over her mouth, and it opens on instinct. My breath hitches and my cock jumps. My cock has been hard since this started in the cave... hell before then. Now it weeps precome just wanting to feel her. I move my hand, pulling her bottom lip down, making her open her mouth even more. Pressing my thumb inside, she sticks her tongue out welcoming it into the warm wet cavern. I growl into her ear as she closes her lips around my digit, swirling her tongue all around it.

I can feel Kyler moving to pull her joggers down her long lean legs and Thomas has moved to sit down next to her pulling the strap of her bra off her shoulder to kiss all along her collarbone, neck and ear. His hand softly grips her tit giving the hardened nipple a slight squeeze. Her back bows slightly and she moans around the digit in her mouth, but I cannot take my eyes from her mouth. She gives it a hard suck and I hiss at the feeling.

Leaning forward, I lick up the side of her neck and nip her ear. "That's right, suck it," I growl into her ear. I feel her whole body tighten at my voice. I know she recognizes it. I look over a Kyler, then Thomas and both of their eyes are glued on her face.

I pull my digit from her lips as Kyler begins to kneed her thighs spreading them further apart. They are spreading for him, so that's a good sign. Her head slowly tilts in my direction, and I give a sinister smile. Her lips are moist from how she was working my thumb over.

"Jay?" she asks, incredulously. Her breathing has increased. I don't know if it's from the revelation or the fact Thomas hasn't stopped his kissing, licking and sucking on her shoulder and neck along with the fondling of her breasts. Or... if its the fact that Kyler has moved even further up her thighs with his massaging ministrations toward the apex of her thighs. We can all smell her arousal now.

"Yeah, Sweetness. It's me," I say, pressing two of my fingers now to her lips. "Now suck my fingers like you want to suck my cock," I growl out as the fingers slip past her open plump lips. It only takes a minute, but she begins swirling her tongue again around and between the fingers sucking them.

I can tell Kyler's patience is wearing thin. He moves the leg closest to Thomas to rest over his leg opening her all the way up. Standing between her thighs, he leans one hand on the back of the couch just over her head, he uses the other to run over her pussy, letting his one finger dip into her folds.

"Fuck, Sky," he growls watching her suck on my fingers. "You're so wet for us. Does it turn you on knowing that we all want to fuck you?" he asks, and she moans louder around my fingers.

Thomas pulls the cups of her lace bra down releasing her full tits over them. He gives the little hard nubs each a pinch. Hissing, she slightly bites down on my fingers, then licks and sucks them to sooth the bite. Fuck, that was hot. And this girl is a virgin? How does she know just what to do?

Pulling my fingers from her lips, I unzip my pants and pull my hard cock from the confines. I notice then that Thomas has her leg that was placed over his thighs in his grasp, looking down where Kyler is slowly rubbing over her glistening pussy.

"Holy hell, Butterfly. You're fucking perfect," I hear him say. Her breathing has increased and as her chest rises and falls her breasts move.

Moving to kneel on the couch, I see Thomas's attention

is pulled to watch me as I shimmy my pants and boxers down a bit on my hips as I turn my body towards the beauty. I stroke my cock a couple of times from root to tip, just to alleviate some tension. Grabbing the hair at the back of her head, she takes in a sharp gasp.

"Open wide, sweetness. We're about to make all your fantasies come true."

She slowly opens her mouth, trusting me just as I knew she would. As I glide my hard cock into her warm mouth, she immediately begins to suck. My fist tightens in her hair, trying to stave off the need to just thrust as far as I can down her throat.

I'm not sure if this is her first time – I sure as fuck hope it is – but she's working her tongue so good for me. "Fuuuuu-uck..." I groan. And now, not only am I wondering if she's done this before, I'm wondering why the fuck I waited so long to do this.

I've been so focused on how well she's sucking me that I didn't even notice Kyler had dropped his pants just like me to his hips. I look up, seeing that he's stroking his cock with his eyes focused on her wet center. With the leg that I'm not kneeling on, I hook it around her other leg, opening her up even more. Making sure she stays spread wide open for us. We want to watch her take his cock for the first time.

He leans low over her as he swipes his cock through her folds getting her wetness all over the head.

"Don't worry, baby girl. I'll be gentle," he says as he roughly rubs his cock over her clit making her jump. "At least in the beginning," he says with a chuckle. She tries to pull away from my cock but I hold her steady.

When he moves to enter her slowly, I pull out of her mouth. She gasps and I can see the frantic look and her heavy breathing. I cup the back of her head, and kiss her deeply, swiping my tongue into her mouth tasting myself on her. She's so rigid right now, but Kyler is moving slowly. Just pumping slightly in and out of her, allowing her to get acclimated to his size.

"Fuck, she's tight," he hisses. When I turn my head to watch even more, I see he's gripping the base of his cock, probably trying to hold off on coming too quickly. She begins shaking her head while she's panting. I can tell she's trying to muster up the courage to tell him no.

"Shhhh... It's okay. It will only hurt for a minute," I say to her. Thomas is still kissing and licking her shoulder and neck but he also started moving down to her tits. Her breathing begins to even out, even though they are still coming in pants. Licking her bottom lip into my mouth, nipping at the tender flesh I notice her tongue moves to greet me. I give her what she needs and kiss her softly with open mouthed kisses, all lips and tongue. It's wet and passionate. My hand moves to cup her breast giving it a little squeeze, then move up to her throat. Holding her tender, lean neck in my grasp, I tighten it a bit but not enough to take away her air. Just enough to let her know I could.

She moans at my hold or it could be that Kyler is getting deeper. "That's it, sweetness. Relax and tell us what you want," I encourage her.

Slowly, Kyler keeps moving in and out, getting deeper and deeper. I'm watching her closely, but I need to see her eyes. I reach up and pull the cloth from her eyes and she blinks her eyes open looking directly into mine. "There you are," I say.

"Jay... please," she begs me so beautifully.

"What do you need?" I ask her. I'm so focused on her, I almost forgot what exactly was going on around me, until she yells shocking me. But she follows it up with a whining moan.

"Yes... belongs to me now... to us," I hear Kyler spit out through grunts making me look down where they are connected. My eyes widen at him moving in and out of her, but what has my full attention is the blood cloating his cock right now. I knew she was a virgin, but this is my first time seeing this. I've never been with a virgin. I've always fucked the popular girls who get around. And never have I gone without protection but with Sky... I want to be buried inside her with nothing between us.

"You're doing so good, sweetness. Such a good girl for us," I say, focusing back on her. I pepper her with compliments as Thomas's hand moves down her body and begins circling her clit. She jolts at the feeling of his hand on her so gentle.

"Oh, god... yes," she breathes and looks down where everything is happening. As soon as her eyes dip to where Kyler is inside of her, he slams inside of her hard making her gasp.

"Look at me, Skylan," Kyler demands holding still deep inside of her. Her eyes immediately fly to his steel grey-blue eyes. The look on his face is feral. This is something he's been holding back just as long as I have. "Mine," he growls out and she nods slowly. I want to correct him, but before I do, he does it for me. "Ours... only ours," he says with a snarl.

Nodding again, a little more emphatic, her breathing is still erratic. He pulls out and slams back in. "Say it!" he barks.

"Yours. All of yours," she says in what could be observed as a yell.

My dick is so fucking hard right now. Placing my index

finger from the hand still around her throat on her cheek, I move her face to look at me. Her eyes glint down to see my hard cock. She sticks her tongue out and I move to slide back into her mouth. I slowly begin to move my cock in and out as she sucks and licks my shaft.

Kyler's face darkens as he grips the back of her thighs that are still spread open for him between mine and Thomas's hold. He begins moving stronger with deeper, harder strokes. "Fuck... feels so fucking good," he grunts through his paces.

Skylan moans around my cock and fucking hell, that feels amazing. The vibrations move all the way up my spine. I know I'm not going to be able to hold on much longer. I release her throat and grasp the messy chestnut hair at the top of her head. I pull out in one quick move, leaning down into her face. Her mouth is still open, but her eyes fly wide to watch me.

"Hold your tongue out," I order and when she complies, I spit on it. "Don't swallow and leave that tongue out. I'm going to fuck your face and you're going to take everything I give you. Do you understand?" I ask. She nods the best she can with me holding her by the hair.

She does just as I say leaving her tongue out. I smile at her, spitting on her tongue once again. I line my cock up to her mouth and let it just run over my saliva slow at first. I don't want to hurt her, but I want her to see how being used can be just as rewarding.

Thomas continues to rub her clit, but between the little circles he does a quick back and forth motion now making her body jerk. Whenever he does that I know her tight little cunt constricts around Kyler's cock because it makes him hiss and stutter his movements.

"Butterfly, you look so sexy right now. Watching you get

fucked by both of them. I want to fuck you so bad," he whispers against her ear loud enough for us to her. She moans even louder making me start to move more inside her mouth to her throat. "You're such a good girl... so fucking good for us. Perfect," Thomas prasises her.

"Fuck, she has a praise kink. She's about to come. I can feel her... she's strangling my dick," Kyler says picking up his pace. He's solely focused on her right now.

"Good girl. Come on Kyler's cock and take everything I'm about to give you," I say above her. I begin fucking even harder into her throat holding her head steady. Her eyes fly open as soon as I hit that spot in the back making her gag reflex tighten her throat up. "That's it, sweetness. Choke on my cock," I growl out.

Her eyes don't leave mine, but they are now flowing with tears streaking down her face. She looks fucking stunning, just like I knew she would. Her back bows as Thomas's hand moves feverishly over her clit.

"That's... it... so fucking tight," Kyler says thrusting deep inside her. His breathing is harsh. He pulls out, continuing to stroke his cock while he spills his seed across her stomach and tits. We're going to have to make sure we get her on birth control as soon as possible if she isn't already. I don't plan to fuck her with a condom and I'm pretty sure Kyler won't either. I'm pretty positive Thomas wouldn't mind, but only because he would only want to do what Skylan wants. He's just a softie like that.

Hearing them both come and watching her gag on my dick, I know I'm about to tip over that edge and choke her on more than my cock.

The gagging sound is getting louder and I feel the electric feeling begin to move up my spine as my balls tighten up. I pull out just slightly as ropes of come coat her tongue and the back of her throat. Pulling out completely, I release the hold on her hair cupping her cheek. Her eyes are so watery, but they never move from mine even though her tongue is still sticking out of her mouth with my come all over it.

"Swallow it," I give a soft demand. She slowly closes her mouth and does just as I ask. I can tell the taste isn't something she was expecting. Leaning over, I gently kiss her lips and watch her eyes flutter close. I swipe my tongue over the seam and she obediently opens, allowing our tongues to twist. Tasting myself on her is making me hard again.

Pulling out of the kiss, I hold her face in both of my palms and press my forehead against hers. She's breathing heavily, and the look she's giving me is exhaustion but contentment. I give a little chuckle. "I know you're tired, but you're not quite done yet," I say to her. She gives a wistful smile while her glassy eyes stare into mine.

My hands move over her shoulders and shift her forward a bit. I untie the cloth that Thomas tied her wrists with. Once she is released, she sinks into the back of the couch, pulling her hands forward rubbing the reddened flesh to massage the soreness. Kyler stands and walks out of the room. Her eyes immediately track his movement.

Looking back to me, her face drops a bit. "Did... did I do something wrong?" she asks, just as he walks back in with a towel from the downstairs bathroom. He leans over her wiping his spunk off her stomach and chest. Her eyes watch him. His brow furrowed but his ministrations cleaning her up is gentle.

I look over at Thomas, as Kyler cleans her and his face is watching every one of her movements. His eyes finally catch mine and I give him a smirk. His brow lifts, and I know he's just wondering if I'm okay with all of this. I am more than okay. As long as Sky is happy and I can have her also, I don't care if my two best friends care about her as well.

Kyler sits down on the coffee table again, leaning his forearms on his thick thighs. He's observing everything and I'm sure he's also still in his head about all of this. Leaning my back against the end of the couch sitting sideways, I look at Thomas and raise my brow. He looks at Skylan this time and leans forward cupping her cheek, pulling her face to his. Her eyes go wide but when his lips touch hers she quickly recovers and kisses him back. Placing one hand on his strong chest, he wraps and arm around her back. Using all his own strength, he guides her to straddle him. I didn't even notice he had his hard cock out already. Probably jacking off while we were fucking her.

Once she's rested over his lap, he cups both of her cheeks and she softly holds his forearms. One glance at Kyler, I know both of us are hard again. I don't think I will ever get enough of her. We're going to have to discuss how this is going to work with our parents now.

He pulls out of the kiss. Staying close to her with their breaths mingling, he speaks softly to her, "If you don't want this... want me... it's okay. Just tell me, butterfly and I will stop."

17

SKYLAN

Staring back into his golden brown orbs is so breathtaking. I've always fantasized about all three of these men, but Thomas... He's been the one who has alway been overly gentle with me. Making sure I'm comfortable, taking care of me in ways that Jayden doesn't. I still can't believe this is what's happening right now.

"Oh Thomas... I'm still trying to figure out if all of this is real," I say on a chuckle. My heart is still erratically beating in my chest and my breathing has just seemed to calm down a bit. Thomas gives a small smile but doesn't laugh.

"It's real, butterfly. And if you want us, we're yours. Now the question is do you want this... want... me?" he asks so low I can barely hear him. When did Thomas ever have a self confidence issue. I've seen the girls he hits on and fucks with. Some a lot better looking than me. More popular. Sexier. I'm still wondering why me?

Lifting my hands to cup his face, pressing my lips softly to his is a kiss that is just a ghosting of our lips. "Bear..." I say using the little nickname I have for him. His cheeks turn a pretty shade of pink and he finally smiles for me. "... I've wanted you for a very long time. I never thought you could ever look at me as more than Jayden's little sister."

"I would never disrespect my friend or our friendship. I've had feelings for you for almost as long as I've known you," he says. I shift closer to press my body even closer, feeling his erection rub against my center, making me moan and him gasp. He's big. Not as big as Kyler, but still huge. "You're fucking killing me here, butterfly."

Looking down, I see his erection is out and he's hard as steel. I'm still wet from my orgasm when Kyler fucked me. Leaning close, I lick the shell of his ear as I purposely rub my soaking wet pussy over his hardness. "Fuck me, Bear," I whisper in his ear and a dark growl comes from his chest. His hand moves from my face to grasp my hips lifting me up. He lines himself up to my core. I'm on my knees over him as we both watch where we're going to be connected in the most primal of ways. Remembering how it felt to be full of Kyler, I wonder if this time if it will hurt again. Or will I only feel the fullness and excitement. This is a different position.

He looks up and since I'm still watching down below, he kisses my forehead. "Take your time. You're in control here," he says, breathing heavily and making me look up at him. I've never done this before. Everything is new to me.

Releasing a heavy shaky breath I start to sink down. He brings his bottom lip into his mouth biting down on it. It stings a bit, but I want this. I want him. I want them all. And here I thought Kyler hated me... and maybe he does, but he also wants me. And I wonder when Jayden started to look at me as more than his little stepsister.

"Fuuuucckkkk," I hear Kyler grit out as he watches me sink lower and lower onto Thomas's cock. I try to focus solely on Thomas but my eyes make their way to Jayden to make sure he's okay with all of this. One look on his face, tells me he's fine with it. He has such a devious smile on his lips and he has his hard cock in his hand as he slowly pleasures himself.

Turning my focus back to Thomas, I lift myself back up and slowly sink down again. Thomas rests his head on the back cushion of the couch, and I think I'm doing something wrong. "I... I don't know... what I'm doing," I whisper and move to cover my blushing face.

Immediately hands grasp my wrists, pulling them away. He pulls me again flush with his body. "Fuck, woman. You're incredible. Your innocence and lack of experience is so fucking sexy. But you need to just do what makes you feel good. Use me," he says.

Placing my hands on his chest, he gently grabs my hips. Lifting me up and slowly bringing me down, he says, "You can ride me like this..." He then pulls my hips forward and pushes me back, making me really moan loudly when my sensitive clit rubs over his pelvis. "... or like that. Or if you really want me to, I can do..." he says as he lifts me up with just a bit of his cock inside me. He holds me there and begins to power thrust up inside me several times. "... this... right... here."

"Oh fuck... oh fuck... oh fu..." I start chanting as I lean further resting my head on his shoulder as his grip on my hips become bruising, but the feeling building inside me makes me really not care about that right now. "Right... there... fuck... keep going... please, Thomas. Don't stop," I say between his thrusts.

"Fuck you're gorgeous. Come for me, beautiful. I want to watch you come apart," he says as the thrusting continues. The intense feeling of a tsunami crests, making me scream and my entire body lock up. He fucks me through the intensity, then pulls me off his cock, sitting me on his thighs shaking as one hand strokes himself through his own orgasm. "We really need to get you on birth control. We're playing fucking Russian Roulette here," he says with a little chuckle.

I look down at the ropes of come striping his muscular chest and abs. Breathing heavily, I look up at him and the smile he graces me with is nothing short of heart-stopping. When I can finally focus on what's going on around us, I look over at Jayden first, and he also has come coating his hand from jerking off. But before I can even look back at Kyler, he grunts. "Looks like we all need a shower now."

Jayden gives a lazy little chuckle. "Good thing our shower upstair is party size."

An hour later, we all are sitting down in the family room again, this time I'm sitting in the corner section of the L-shaped couch, with Kyler on one side of me, Jayden on the other and Thomas is sitting on the floor just below me. He didn't want to be outdone since the other two were sitting right next to me.

"So..." I say, wringing my hands in my lap. Kyler is leaning back casually, Jayden is half laying down with his leg thrown over the end of the couch, his shoulder pressed against mine, and Thomas is sitting sideways looking up at me. This is Jayden and my usual way of watching television or a movie at home, but now this feels more intimate. He's staring at me, just as other two are.

"So, what?" Kyler says a little harshly. This is what I mean, he hates me. Looking down in my lap, I really just want to go to my room now. I feel stupid. Tears welling in my eyes, but I do all I can to make sure they don't fall.

Feeling a hand touch my knee, I look up and I see it's Jayden. My eyes rise to his. "Hey," he says quietly. "Tell me what's on your mind. Ignore Ky."

"Fuck off, Jay," I hear Kyler mumble under his breath. But I do just as Jayden suggests and focus on him, ignoring Kyler's little outburst.

"I don't know. I just feel like... I guess... is this real?" I ask, looking at my stepbrother. He gives me a soft smile.

"This is real, if you want it to be real. Is this something you want?" he questions me. Maybe that's why Kyler is upset. He was just looking for a little fun for the holiday but doesn't want anything else. From what Thomas said earlier, he wants to be with me, so I know or at least I hope he wants this to be real.

"What about our parents, Jay? Are you sure about this?" I turn the question on him. Finally, moving slowly he sits up facing me. Pulling one of my hands into his lap, he looks me in the eye.

"If you want to do this, sweetness, I will handle our parents. We aren't blood related so there's nothing they can say there. But before we fight that fight, I need to be sure you're all in," he says, looking a little nervous.

Looking down at our clasped hands, I try to figure out how to tell him how I feel. It's so hard putting your heart on the line to the one you've always been able to turn to, more so in front of his best friends. "I never knew something like this...," I say, looking back up at him and motioning between us with my free hand. "Something with you, was possible. Let alone with any of you. Of course, I'm all in. I'm just really hoping I'm not the only one."

Releasing my hands, he cups my face and leans in

kissing my lips softly. Not deep, just little pecks. "Skylan James... we have argued and fought, but I have always been right by your side. That will never change. The only thing that will change is that I'm now completely yours," he says with a serious face. The deep timbre of his voice brooks no argument from me. I can't take my eyes from his gorgeous milk chocolate ones.

Giving a small smile, I place my hands over his still cupping my face and nod. "I want this Jay. More than anything, I want this right here," I say with confidence in my voice.

"Good," he replies and once again kisses my lips. Just below us on the floor, Thomas clears his throat in attempt to probably break the spell Jayden and I are in. Chuckling, I drop my hands and so does Jayden, but he entwines one of our hands like he just doesn't want to stop touching me. It's a strange change to our dynamic, but one I'm not at all running from.

Reaching down I tousle Thomas's golden locks, making him smile. "Butterfly, you already know I'm all in. Especially with Jayden finally giving me his permission and not threatening to kill me," he says making me guffaw with a laugh. Glancing over, I see Jayden roll his eyes but give a little laugh.

"Yeah, you have my blessing... but you hurt her and you already know what's coming for you, right?" Jayden says, in a more serious voice. Thomas's playfulness disappears with talk of hurting me. Thomas sits up even more, throwing an arm over my lap, gripping my thigh, but never taking his eyes off of Jayden.

"I would expect nothing less, and even invite it if I do, however, I don't plan to ever hurt Skylan. I've already told you that my feelings for her run deep," he says, making me a bit breathless. He talked to Jayden about this already. Thomas and I will need to sit down one on one to discuss this more in depth, but for right now, we're just laying down the groundwork for the "relationship".

Jayden nods his head, bringing his fist out to which Thomas does the same and they bump them. "Then you're good with me. You already know I trust you with her. I only trust her around you and Kyler..." Jayden's voice teeters off, and we all hesitantly look to where Kyler sits.

The dark haired greek god sits there focusing on his lap. He's leaning away from me, I'm guessing trying to be in the conversation just far enough away from me. One arm is thrown over the back of the couch to appear casual, yet his body is rigid and the furrow in his brow says he is anything but casual or relaxed.

"Ky," Jayden barks out, making the divot in his forehead increase. He still doesn't look up and I don't know why I expected anything other than hostility from him. My eyes drop back down to mine and Jayden's entwined hands.

Time seems to drag on with the staring contest that seems to be happening here. Both Jayden and Thomas staring at Kyler right now. The intensity in the air is stifling and all I want to do is get away.

Moving to stand up, I say, "How about I go make–" But I'm interrupted.

"I don't know..." Kyler starts but then breaks off shaking his head. Releasing a deep sigh, he slowly lifts his gaze to meet my eyes. "I don't know how to be in a relationship nor have I ever been in one, Sky. But..."

Relaxing back into the couch, I shift my body to face him more. It's a little difficult with Thomas between my legs and his arm resting over my thigh, but I do the best I can. "But what?" I ask quietly. I don't want to pressure him, but now I'm curious. His harsh tone doesn't match his words, so I wonder if this is normal for him.

"But... I want to try for you," he says. The look on his face seems to relay he's either angry or very conflicted right now. "I just don't know how."

Giving a small gentle smile, I release the breath I had been holding. All this time, I never thought in a thousand years would I be able to have a relationship with one of these guys, let alone all three, but here we are trying to work out the specifics and guidelines. And we have the next two weeks to do it without the interruption of our parents or any other obligations.

"Ky... I don't know how either. I've never been in a relationship. But I'm sure we can figure it out. Together," I say. We stare at one another for what feels like an eternity. "I'm willing to work through everything... if you are?" I question.

Kyler sits up, scooting a little closer to us and nods. I can see Thomas and Jayden smiling at one another out of my periphery.

"So are we doing this for real then?" Jayden asks, giving my hand a little squeeze. Glancing between all three of these gorgeous men, my heart feels so full and content.

"I'm all in, if you guys are. I want this... especially if I get more of the masked men again," I say laughing. The guys chuckle, Thomas louder than the others. Kyler just stares at me.

"Seriously? You would do that again?" Kyler asks me, making me nod furiously.

"Holy shit, yeah. That was hot. I was scared a little but turned on like crazy," I reply.

"Then you're ours, Skylan James. And now no one will ever take you from us," Jayden says lifting my hand to his lips, kissing my knuckles making me blush slightly.

Kyler reaches over, to take my other hand in his. He lifts it, palm up, to kiss the inside of my wrist, making a shiver run through me. "No one, baby girl. You're ours," he says.

My smile is so wide, and I feel so full. Feeling Thomas squeeze my thigh once again, I look down into his smirking face. "Forever, Butterfly," Thomas says.

"Forever," I reply.

ACKNOWLEDGMENTS

Acknowledgements

First and foremost, I want to thank Melissa McSherry and Tyla Rae, for always being the constant encouragement. Always pushing me to continue and keep going, when all I want to do is sleep. Both of you in my DM's keeping me sane and you have both been my lifeline for sure.

A huge thank you to my betas (and friends) who helped make this what it is, Amanda Eastling, CJ Riggs and Justine Capraro. You guys rock! Always helping and also encouraging me just when I need it.

Thank you to the authors who continue to inspire me everyday. Most of these are my one-click authors, and if you haven't read them yet... what are you waiting for. I hope one day I will be considered just half as great as you guys. Shantel Tessier, Siobhan Davis, BJ Alpha, Santana Knox, Melody Mode, Nikki J. Summers, Yolanda Olson, Nova Kane, Kinsley Kincaid, NJ Weeks, Angel Lawson and Amo Jones!

Last but definitely not least, a huge thank you to a few very special people who have known from the beginning about my writing journey. They encouraged and supported me in every way they could. From keeping the secret to cheering me on, they were always there in my DM's, on phone calls and even little coffee dates; Chanel Johnson, Cassie Weaver, Keeley Witham, Heather Rada, Christine Harris, Stephanie Hutchinson, Tabitha Johnson, Cady Cyr, Meagan Kerr and my biggest cheerleaders of all, my son, Skyler James Rivera and my daughter, Tia Justice Rivera.

22664009R00097